"He has my n
whispered ho
very much lik~~e baby pictures of~~
me."

"Surprise, surprise," Gaby said dryly as she bent down to lift the child, who was already holding his arms up in anticipation. "I did tell you he was yours."

Angel tensed as she spun back around to face him. He wasn't comfortable with young children. None of his friends had kids yet. Nobody handed him a baby and expected him to know what to do with it...but Gaby *did*. She plonked Alexios into Angel's arms as though he were a parental veteran.

Angel stared into those vivid green eyes that reminded him so disturbingly of his late mother. His son smiled and planted a chubby little hand against the stubble surrounding Angel's mouth, fingers exploring that interesting roughness. The baby giggled.

That innocent chuckle released Angel's tension. A smile flashed across his wide, sensual mouth and Gaby's heart stuttered in receipt of that powerful flare of raw masculine charisma...

Heirs for Royal Brothers

When one night with a prince has life-changing consequences!

Royal half brothers Prince Saif Basara of Alharia and Prince Angelino Diamandis of Themos are both scarred by the dramatic circumstances of their births. Their upbringings might have been very different, but they are united in one key goal—to never fall in love!

But fate has other plans when the guarded brothers meet their matches in Tatiana Hamilton and Gabriella Knox. And only a royal wedding will do when there are royal heirs involved!

Read Saif and Tatiana's story in
Cinderella's Desert Baby Bombshell

Read Angelino and Gabriella's story in
Her Best Kept Royal Secret

Both available now!

Lynne Graham

—

HER BEST KEPT ROYAL SECRET

Recycling programs
for this product may
not exist in your area.

ISBN-13: 978-1-335-56898-4

Her Best Kept Royal Secret

Copyright © 2021 by Lynne Graham

All rights reserved. No part of this book may be used or reproduced in
any manner whatsoever without written permission except in the case of
brief quotations embodied in critical articles and reviews.

This is a work of fiction. Names, characters, places and incidents
are either the product of the author's imagination or are used fictitiously.
Any resemblance to actual persons, living or dead, businesses,
companies, events or locales is entirely coincidental.

This edition published by arrangement with Harlequin Books S.A.

For questions and comments about the quality of this book,
please contact us at CustomerService@Harlequin.com.

Harlequin Enterprises ULC
22 Adelaide St. West, 40th Floor
Toronto, Ontario M5H 4E3, Canada
www.Harlequin.com

Printed in U.S.A.

Lynne Graham was born in Northern Ireland and has been a keen romance reader since her teens. She is very happily married to an understanding husband who has learned to cook since she started to write! Her five children keep her on her toes. She has a very large dog who knocks everything over, a very small terrier who barks a lot and two cats. When time allows, Lynne is a keen gardener.

Books by Lynne Graham

Harlequin Presents

The Greek's Convenient Cinderella
The Ring the Spaniard Gave Her

Cinderella Brides for Billionaires

Cinderella's Royal Secret
The Italian in Need of an Heir

Heirs for Royal Brothers

Cinderella's Desert Baby Bombshell

Innocent Christmas Brides

A Baby on the Greek's Doorstep
Christmas Babies for the Italian

Visit the Author Profile page
at Harlequin.com for more titles.

CHAPTER ONE

'WHEN AM *I* going to marry?' Angelino Dia-mandis rolled his dark heavily lashed eyes with slumbrous amusement in receipt of his brother's question.

Christened Angel by his friends, it being an in-joke that he was anything but angelic, the ruling Prince of Themos sprawled back on the upholstered ottoman in an untidy but in-disputably graceful tangle of long lean limbs and simply smiled over his cup of coffee. The movie-star good looks that had long made him a favourite of the paparazzi had rarely been more breathtakingly obvious.

Prince Saif of Alharia, clad in the tradi-tional silk finery of a bridegroom, studied his younger half-brother with an unimpressed frown. 'Why are you smiling? As though I had asked you something foolish? You are a head of state and one day, just like me, you must marry. Neither of us has a choice.'

That last statement was voiced without resentment or self-pity, Angel acknowledged, wryly amused by his brother's heartfelt sense of duty and honour. Saif still rejoiced in a streak of naivety that Angel had never had. Saif had been surrounded from birth by all the safety barriers a devoted elderly father considered necessary to conserve his only son's happiness and security.

Angel, in comparison, had never known either parental love or parental protectiveness although he had never admitted that to a living soul. He had been raised by servants and sent to boarding school, his parents much craved but distant figures on his horizon... until he'd gained the maturity to see what they were *really* like. Catching his mother in bed with his best friend at the age of fifteen had been a cruel wake-up call to reality, and being exposed to his father's equally grubby activities had been crushing. He had learned that all the money, privilege and status in the world couldn't compensate for an essential lack of decency and good taste.

Angel had, however, left his brother with his innocent illusions intact about the mother who had abandoned him and her first husband, the Emir of Alharia, to run off with Angel's father. Queen Nabila and her equally self-indulgent second husband, King Achilles, had, after all, died in a helicopter crash when Angel was sixteen. There was no good reason now to tell Saif the ugly truth about the mother he had never known.

'Not much choice when it comes to marrying,' Angel conceded ruefully. 'But I still wouldn't have agreed to go into an arranged marriage with a bride I haven't met, as you have done.'

'You *know* the precarious state of my father's health.'

'I do, but I also think you will eventually have to stop tiptoeing around him.'

Saif stiffened defensively. 'You say that because I have not yet had the courage to tell my father about my relationship with you… and I've hidden you away here in a forgotten part of the palace to conceal your presence in Alharia on my wedding day.'

Angel nodded gently. 'We are not children who need to hide wrongdoing,' he murmured wryly. 'Our mother grievously betrayed your father, but our blood tie should not be denied because of her behaviour.'

Saif looked troubled, too honest a man to deny that fact. 'In time I will tell him that we have a sibling relationship.'

Annoyed that he had taken his bad mood

out on his serious older brother by reproaching him, Angel changed the subject. 'I will not be entering an arranged marriage as such when I wed but I have already chosen my bride.'

'You are in love?' Saif flashed him a sudden smile of mingled surprise and approval. 'I had not thought you would even recognise that possibility.'

'And you were right,' Angel interposed. 'I'm not in love and neither would Cassia be. She is simply the most suitable woman I know to take on the role of Queen, although to be frank I have not yet discussed the subject with her. It is merely that I know her practical views on marriage. Status and wealth appeal most to her.'

'Cassia!' Saif sliced in, his consternation unhidden because he had clearly been taken by surprise by that familiar name. 'That *frozen* blonde?' Breaking off mid-sentence, Saif reddened at his lack of tact and compressed his lips shut again before concluding, 'Forgive me… I was—'

Angel shifted a dismissive hand and laughed with genuine appreciation. 'No, Cassia and the iceberg that sank the *Titanic* do have much in common,' he responded equably. 'But that's the type of wife I would prefer.

I don't want an emotionally incontinent bride or a demanding one or one likely to be unfaithful or careless of appearances. Cassia will suit me and my needs as the ruler of Themos very well indeed. Our sole challenge would be the production of an heir because I don't think she is a very physical woman, but no doubt we would deal with that requirement when the time arrives…and neither of us would be in any hurry to get to the altar. I am only twenty-eight and she is twenty-five. According to our constitution, I cannot be crowned King until I marry or produce an heir.'

Saif dealt him a remarkably sombre look. 'Such a bloodless arrangement won't work for you, Angel. You have much more heart than you are prepared to admit. Even if Cassia seems the perfect candidate now, at some stage of your life you will want *more*,' he declared.

Angel simply laughed again, utterly unconvinced by that sentimental forecast, indeed, only his respect for his brother killing the scornful rebuttal ready to leap to his tongue. He had never been in love in his life, and he didn't believe he was capable of that kind of self-delusion. It was his belief that love was more often the excuse for the dreadful things that people did. His mother had told him that it had been her love for his father that had made her desert her first husband. Of course, she hadn't even mentioned the infant son she had left behind at the same time, he recalled in disgust, or the fact that she had already been pregnant with Angel by Prince Achilles. Too often, Angel had seen friends treat each other badly and employ love as a justification for cheating, lying and betraying the trusting or the innocent. He was a realist. He knew exactly what sort of marriage he would be getting if he wed a woman like Cassia and that brand of icy detachment would suit him to perfection.

'I must return to the reception.' Saif sighed with regret. 'I am very sorry that you are unable to join the festivities.'

Setting his cup aside, Angel vaulted fluidly upright. 'No, you were right to hide me,' he said softly. 'I was, as I often can be, impulsive in flying out here the instant you told me you were getting married. For sure, someone would have recognised me at the party.'

His brother gave him a discomfited look and Angel suppressed a sigh but there was nothing he could do to change the situation. He, the child of their mother's scandalous second marriage, could not expect to be a welcome guest in the Emir's family circle. Some

day, of course, that would change when nature
took its course and the elderly Emir passed,
but it was unlikely to change any sooner.
Angel rejected the faint sense of resentment
afflicting him as he accompanied his brother
out to the open galleried corridor beyond the
suite of rooms where he had been placed. The
palace of Alharia was a vast building, built
over many centuries and capable of hiding
an army should there be that necessity, he
thought wryly, glancing over the wall into the
courtyard beneath and catching a glimpse of
red hair that spun his head back.

'Who's that?' he heard himself ask of the
woman below, playing with a ball and a couple of young children.

'Haven't a clue,' Saif admitted. 'By the look
of that starchy uniform, someone's nanny…
she probably belongs to one of our wedding
guests.'

Belongs? Just as if the woman were a stray
dog, Angel savoured with amusement. Was he
quite as remote from the domestic staff as his
elder brother appeared to be? He didn't think
so. His childhood had put paid to that lofty
royal distance. The only affection he had ever
received had come from his parents' employees and he had learned to think of them and

see them as individuals rather than mere servants there to ensure his comfort.

'It was the red hair. It always catches my eye,' Angel confided truthfully, still looking down into the courtyard while censuring himself for doing so.

Obviously, it wasn't *her*! As bright as she had been at Cambridge when he met her, there was no way she would now, five years on, be as humbly employed as a nanny in service. And why hadn't he long since forgotten about that wretched girl? With her combat boots, stroppy attitude and blue eyes deeper and truer in colour than even the legendary Diamandis sapphires? He gritted his teeth in annoyance at the vagaries of his persistent memories. Was it because she had been the one who, in popular parlance, had got away? Was he still that basic? That male and predictable?

'Yes…that's very noticeable,' Saif remarked with a hint of amusement. 'You are an unrepentant womaniser, Angel. Everything the global tabloids say about you is true but at least you have enjoyed the freedom to be yourself.'

'And so will you some day.' Angel gave his brother's shoulder a quick consoling pat even while he knew that he was voicing a white lie intended to comfort. As an obedient son, most probably a *very* faithful husband and the future emir of a traditional country, Saif was unlikely to ever have the liberty to do as he liked, but there was little point in reminding him of that hard fact, Angel reasoned with sympathy.

Luckily for Angel, his subjects didn't expect moral perfection from their monarch. The island of Themos in the Mediterranean Sea was a liberal and independent nation. Although it was a small country, Themos was also incredibly rich because it was a tax haven, beloved of the wealthy and famous for many affluent generations. The royal family of Diamandis was of Greek origin and had ruled Themos since the fifteenth century. Throughout history Angel's wily family had retained the throne through judicious alliances with more powerful nations and, while their army might be small, their formidable financial holdings ensured that Themos would always box above its weight.

Angel studied what he could see of the nanny, the gleam of that fiery hair displayed in a simple long braid visible beneath the woven sun hat she wore. In the sunlight that braid glittered like polished copper, summoning up further uninvited echoes from the past.

Squaring his wide shoulders as he separated from his brother, Angel turned away and returned to the suite that had been put at his disposal, a glossy concealment of the truth that he was under virtual house arrest until he flew out of Alharia again because his brother didn't want him to be seen and recognised.

Regrettably, Angel hadn't realised that *that* would be a problem. He had assumed that the wedding ceremony would be a hugely crowded public event, not a strictly private affair with only the Emir and the bride's parents in attendance. He had arrived for the wedding with the comforting belief that there would be so many people present that he would easily escape detection. The discovery that he could not attend either ceremony or reception had exasperated him. As an adult, Angel had little experience of disappointment and certainly not the boredom of hiding out alone in Victorian surroundings, far removed from the comforts he took for granted. He wasn't a 'kick back and watch television' kind of person, he reasoned irritably, but it *was* only for a few hours. He reached for his phone as it vibrated.

It was the pilot of his private jet. A fault had been discovered in the landing-gear hydraulics. Angel winced even as he was assured that the mechanics team that had already flown in would be working on the problem through the night in an effort to get him airborne and back home again as soon as possible. He swore under his breath and paced the Persian carpet below his feet, wondering what he could possibly do to pass the time...

Gabriella flicked through the television channels again in search of entertainment, but it was no use. Even though she spoke the language, nothing she had so far seen could capture her attention.

In an effort to dispel her bleak mood, she stood up, stretching in the light white cotton sundress she had donned once the sun went down, and her official workday was over. Not that she had had the opportunity to do any *real* work during her brief stay in Alharia, she reflected wryly. Having registered her services with an international nanny agency the month before, Gaby was only accepting short-term placements. A couple of bad experiences in more permanent positions had made her wary and she intended to be far more cautious when choosing her next live-in employer. Providing childcare cover for wedding guests in the Alharian royal palace had sounded like a ridiculously exciting, glamorous and *safe* job.

Only in actuality the experience, while certainly safe, had proved to be anything but exciting and glamorous. Tired of sitting around doing nothing, she was counting the hours until her flight home the following day.

Aside from an hour in the afternoon spent supervising two six-year-olds, she hadn't *had* any children to look after because most of the guests had either left their kids at home or had brought their own staff with them. Someone had overlooked that likelihood when hiring her and she had been surplus to requirements. So, what else is new? she asked herself with faint bitterness. Being an unwanted extra was a painfully familiar sensation for Gabriella.

Her parents and her little brother had died in a motorway pile-up when she was fourteen years old and recalling the sudden savagery of that shattering loss could still make her skin turn cold and clammy. Grief had shot her straight from awkward adolescence into scary adulthood long before she was ready for the challenge. Her mother's kid sister, Janine, had become Gaby's reluctant guardian and virtually all the money that her parents had left had been used to pay for the fancy boarding school that had kept her out of Janine's hair. She had received a terrific education at the cost of the love, security and healing that she had needed so much more. Barely a year after losing her parents and brother she had decided that she would concentrate on becoming a top-flight nanny, after graduating from university. In her innocence, she had assumed that living in a family situation would ease her heartache for the family she had lost.

Only, Gaby reflected with deep sadness, she had been far too young and ignorant of the world when she had made that decision. Unhappily, the job hadn't worked out the way she had hoped and now she was wondering whether she should be looking at a different career option. Thankfully, she did have the qualifications required to seek an alternative. Gifted from birth, Gaby spoke six languages fluently and had a working knowledge of several more along with a first-class degree in Modern Languages from Cambridge University. The prospect of looking for a starter job in another field held little appeal for her, however, when she was able to earn an excellent salary in the job she was in. Sadly, though, her recent experiences as a nanny had sapped her confidence and left her feeling more alone than ever. Should she fight through that feeling? she asked herself as she lifted her soft drink and wandered out to the courtyard outside her room.

Colourful glass lanterns burned below the loggia that ringed all four sides. Tall fluffy palm trees cast giant shadows across the terracotta floor tiles and the fountain gently spraying water down into a circular pond. The warm still air was infused with the fragrance of exotic flowers, and the sound of the falling water was soothing. There was nothing glamorous about the old-fashioned nursery she had spent her day in, the few people she had met or her small unadorned bedroom, but the courtyard was a truly beautiful place.

She sat down on a stone bench, determined to appreciate her surroundings because tomorrow she would be returning to London and searching for somewhere to live again. She didn't want to overstay in her aunt's spare room. She and Janine had never been close. A fresh live-in position would make practical sense, but she could only grimace at the prospect and as she lifted her head and straightened her tense shoulders in denial of that awful surge of anxiety her long loose hair shimmied round her in rippling waves. Nobody was ever going to scare her like that again, she promised herself fiercely, but the fear that someone might try to do so still lingered…

Angel saw her from the walkway above,

but she was seated in the shadow of the trees. Only a pale gleaming pair of shapely lower legs was visible from his vantage point. A confident half-smile tilting his wide sensual mouth, he strode down the corner staircase and saw her in the light shed by the lanterns, her metallic copper hair shimmering in a glorious tumble of bright splendour. Angel stopped dead. He had a 'thing' for redheads because of a young student who had had hair exactly like that and he was immediately gripped by an intense sense of familiarity.

But it could not be Gabriella Knox, it wasn't possible, he reasoned with a frown of disbelief, his keen dark gaze narrowing as he stared across the courtyard at her, and instantly fierce recognition fired inside him. That nanny he had glimpsed earlier? It *had* been her. It *was* her! His focus now considerably more intent, he appraised her in search of change and found little evidence of the years that had passed.

Possibly that oval face of hers was a little finer now that she had reached her twenties, he reasoned, but, if anything, she was even more of a beauty than she had been at nineteen. Her hair was spectacular, and the delicate cast of her features was only accentuated by her fair, flawless skin. She was a little on the small side, indeed barely five feet two inches in height, but that did not dim Angel's appreciation of her other charms. The average man might first notice Gaby's hair and her face, but her highly feminine curvaceous figure commanded equal attention. Five years earlier those wondrous curves of hers had infiltrated his every fantasy.

Back then, he had quantified Gabriella's appeal, pigeonholed her and rationalised his attraction to her because right from the start she had been trouble and Angel had never in his life before or since chased trouble in his sex life. He didn't take risks; he didn't *need* to take risks. Women were invariably all too willing to agree to his smallest wish…only *not* Gabriella. Gabriella had stood firm, defying him to the last.

Yet in his opinion what he had asked for had not been unreasonable. Other women hadn't argued, most certainly hadn't accused him of trying to steal their freedom or control them. He had an understandable need for discretion in the women he took as lovers. But Gabriella had been too outspoken, volatile and independent to agree to his rules. Encounters with women who only wanted to bed him to sell a story to the paparazzi had educated Angel the hard way and, while the great and good of Themos couldn't care less that their ruling prince might have remarkable staying power between the sheets, Angel held himself accountable to a higher standard than either of his parents had observed. He believed that revelations in print about his sex life were seedy and undignified.

'Gabriella...' Angel murmured tautly.

Gaby was frozen in fear when she glimpsed a dark male silhouette at the edge of the courtyard, but then fear turned into incredulous recognition. Shock kept her locked to the stone bench. Initially she was unable to credit that it could be Angel, but being forced to accept that it *was* him could only horrify her. Meeting Angel again plunged her into a nightmare of mortification, forcing her back into the painful insecurities of her younger self.

For the space of a crazy few weeks, she had once been madly in love with Angel Diamandis, but he had made unreasonable demands and torn her tender heart to pieces. Subsequently, he had shown neither remorse nor regret. After a massive fight in which she had screamed at him and thrown things, it had all been over, her pride's sole consolation being that she had dumped him and refused to listen to his excuses. They had certainly not parted as friends and she had been grateful when he had finished his degree and returned home to Themos, so that she need not continue seeing him around.

'Angel…' Her strained voice emerged somewhere between a whisper and a croak.

He was so very tall, at least six feet three inches and built with all the classic muscular power of an athlete, broad shoulders and strong chest tapering down to a narrow waist and long, powerful legs. When had she forgotten just how tall he was? In a dark, exquisitely cut designer suit, he was as elegant and classy as he had always been. With every breath that he drew, Angel exuded sophistication, royal pedigree and immeasurable wealth. Even casually clad in jeans he had been an arresting sight, she conceded as he stalked closer, his striking grace of movement holding her attention more than she liked. She hated him, she reminded herself, so why was she staring at him like a rabbit mesmerised by headlights? Of course, five long years on, she didn't want to *still* be showing hostility, she reflected in dismay, her cheeks warming, because wouldn't that kind of oversensitivity only encourage his voracious ego? Be calm, be cool, be polite, she urged herself in desperation.

He moved closer and the lights edging the path illuminated him to gleam lovingly over hard slashed cheekbones set high beneath olive skin, and shadow deep-set dark-as-coal eyes before glimmering across the sculpted lines of his wide, sensual mouth. He was still beautiful in a way she had never known a man could be and he still inexorably took her breath away. The very first time she had seen him she had been unable to *stop* looking at him and she had tripped over her own feet and fallen down a step, bruising and cutting her knees. Blood had seeped from the wounds as she'd fought the angry tears stinging her eyes for the pain she had inflicted on herself from clumsy inattention. It had not occurred to her in that moment, or to anyone else, that Angel would simply stride across the court-yard, scoop her up into his arms and take her away for coffee and a clean-up as if such care from a stranger were the most normal thing in the world. But then, that Samaritan act had been pure Angel, reacting to a stray impulse and utterly unpredictable.

'I suppose you are one of the wedding guests,' Gaby surmised, dredging herself up out of the depth of memories that threatened to drown her. She was rather pleased at the level tone of her voice, which suggested that his sudden appearance was not fazing her at all.

'Something like that.' Angel shrugged as only he could do, a graceful shift of a broad shoulder that was continental, eloquent and highly sophisticated in its dismissal. 'But what are *you* doing in the Alharian palace?'

'It would be lovely to sit here and catch up,' Gaby declared with a fake smile pinned to her lips as she rose hurriedly to her feet. 'But I'm tired and I was just about to return to my room for an early night.'

'You can't *still* be that angry with me!' Angel shot at her in sheer wonderment.

Gaby stiffened and lifted her chin, denying the hot colour of embarrassment she could feel flooding into her cheeks. 'Of course not.'

'Then be normal and join me for a drink.'

'I don't think that would be appropriate,' Gaby parried uncomfortably.

'Since when did I do appropriate?' Angel mocked. 'Don't be a killjoy. Seeing you again here after so many years is a hell of a coincidence and, since we both seem to be at a loose end, why shouldn't we catch up?'

Gaby gritted her teeth on an acerbic retort, which would be all too revealing to a guy as shrewd as Angel. What he didn't know about women hadn't yet been written. He was the biggest playboy in Europe, a living legend of a womaniser. She had her pride, of course she had, and the last thing she wanted him to suspect was that she was still prickly about what had happened between them when they were both students... For goodness' sake, how juvenile would that be? she scolded herself frantically, desperate to take control of the encounter. It was not even as though they had had an actual relationship back then. They had shared a couple of dates and it had been over before it even properly began between them.

'Why not?' she agreed without looking at him, belatedly recalling that he was a prince and that even when he was a student his circle of friends had made a point of always addressing him with the very proper title 'Your Highness' or 'sir', and that they had visibly winced for her every time she'd neglected to employ the same honorific. It hadn't been a deliberate omission, though. The reminders of his true status had always come as a surprise to her because, when they were alone together, he had told her to call him Angel and she would always forget who he really was.

She had forgotten because she needed to forget who he was to be with him in *any* way. A royal prince when she was ordinary. A very rich young man when she lived from hand to mouth, a perennially broke student. A sexual sophisticate when she was still a virgin. But she had closed her eyes to reality because she had wanted desperately to *be* with him, only she had not been quite desperate enough to sign away her legal rights at his request! And when she had told him *no*, a word Angel had had very little experience of hearing and no prayer of ever accepting, he had gone off in search of a more accessible and accommodating woman, keen to do whatever it took to be with him, even if the resulting fling would only last a couple of weeks. The longevity of Angel's interest in a woman lasted about as long as a snowflake falling in summer.

Quieting those turbulent memories while struggling to recover her composure, Gaby accompanied Angel up the stairs in the corner. 'Where are you taking me?' she asked.

'My suite is on the floor above.'

A *suite*, well, that was only to be expected given his status in comparison to her own. 'I'm surprised we're in the same wing,' she confided. 'This seems to be a rather out-of-the-way corner of the palace and I understand why *I* was put here because children can be noisy.'

'I was a last-minute guest and a late arrival,'

Angel slotted in, his explanation smooth as glass.

He was lying. Gaby didn't know why he was lying about something so trivial, but five years earlier she had worked out that Angel was at his most smooth and lazy in tone when he wasn't telling the whole truth, when he was probably bending it for her benefit or his own. He was coldly logical, manipulative, indeed far too clever for his own good, and yet his flaws had inexplicably fascinated her far more than they had repelled her. He had tried to run rings around her and impress her with his wealth and she had stood back watching, involuntarily intrigued by that Machiavellian intellect of his as he tried to discover her weakness and use it against her.

'What do children have to do with your presence here in Alharia?' Angel enquired, pressing open a door that mercifully led not into a bedroom as she had feared, but into a spacious sitting room.

'I work as a nanny. This was a short booking.'

'You surprise me.'

'I'm extremely well paid and I enjoy the travel,' she said lightly, determined to reveal nothing private. 'Where are your bodyguards? I thought you never travelled without them.'

'I have no need of bodyguards in a palace as well guarded as this one.' Angel had left his security team behind in a city hotel because an entourage would only have drawn more attention to him. 'What would you like to drink?'

'I thought alcohol was forbidden here?'

'No, it's not. The Emir merely disapproves but he doesn't limit his guests. There are chilled wines available,' Angel murmured, studying her with narrowed eyes of appreciation, well aware that she would slap him if she knew that he was looking at her when her thin cotton dress was transparent against the light.

She wasn't wearing a bra and he could see everything from the colour of her white panties to the lush swell of small full breasts crowned with prominent pink nipples. He very much enjoyed that view. As a dulled throb pulsed at his groin he dragged his attention from her again, mocking himself for being so very easily aroused. As a man accustomed to topless-bathing beauties, why was he getting hard as a rock at the shadowy glimpse of a nipple? He marvelled at his lack of discipline and wondered if he could put it down to the complete shock of seeing Gabriella again. She unsettled him and he didn't like that.

'Rosé…or white wine. Either will do,' Gaby declared, walking across the room because she felt very self-conscious standing there like a statue. She settled down on a satin-covered gilded sofa that was not conducive to relaxation and lifted her chin, striving to appear composed and uninterested at the same time. 'So, catching up?'

Keen to avoid the pitfalls of a too-personal conversation with Gabriella, Angel rolled his memory back several years. 'Whatever happened to those two best friends of yours? The blonde twins?'

It was a winning question, marvellously uncontroversial, he registered as a sudden smile of surprise chased the tension from her plump pink lips. Most women he knew became competitive and curt if he enquired after any other female, convinced that only they should have his attention, but Gabriella was remarkably generous in that line. 'Liz and Laurie?' she queried. 'They both trained as teachers and now they're married.'

'Married?' Angel stressed in astonishment. 'At your age?'

'And Liz has already had her first child,' Gaby completed calmly. 'A little boy. He's so cute.'

Angel winced as if such fond talk of children were in some way embarrassing. 'You always liked kids, so I suppose I shouldn't be surprised that you decided to work with them, but there is so much more in the world.'

'Wine, men and song aren't really my style,' Gaby said drily, her attention locked to him in spite of her efforts to look away.

But there Angel stood, a living, breathing magnet for female attention. It was as if he sucked all the oxygen out of a room when she looked at him because she could barely swallow, and her mouth was dry. She still struggled to credit that a man could be as breathtakingly handsome as he was without being excessively vain or making the smallest effort to impress. She remembered the extraordinary efforts other women had made to grab his attention at university and reminded herself that she had not been one of them.

Angel flashed a sizzling smile at her as he uncorked a bottle of wine and poured it. 'I wondered how long it would take you to make an insulting remark about my reputation.'

Gaby went pink and lifted her chin as he crossed the room to extend a wine glass to her. 'You're reading something into my response that wasn't intended.'

Angel grinned as if she was hugely amusing him. 'You're so full of prejudice that you don't even see it. Instead of acknowledging the attraction between us, you look for an excuse to write me off. It was always like that. You never gave me a fair chance.'

Infuriated by that condemnation, Gaby leapt upright. 'I—'

'And now you're going to shout loudly at me and throw things to make sure that you can't *hear* anything that you don't want to hear,' Angel forecast, smooth as glass.

Gaby could feel temper mushrooming up inside her like an explosion and she swallowed it back while her hands closed into tight fists of restraint. Angel gazed back at her, dark eyes flaming like golden torches of challenge, and she sat down again abruptly, refusing to fulfil his low expectations of her.

'I think I've grown up a little more than that,' Gaby murmured stiffly, her spine rigid, her chest still heaving as she battled to get her temper back under control. No man had ever driven her to such immediate rage as Angel did. He had a special knack in that department. They were oil and water or hay and a lit match, she conceded heavily.

'Prove it,' Angel invited, striving not to let his attention be drawn by the shimmying swell of her sumptuous breasts below the cotton. 'Enjoy your wine. Talk to me.'

CHAPTER TWO

'WHAT DO YOU want to talk about?' Gaby asked very drily and sipped at her wine.

'Tell me what it is like being a nanny,' Angel invited, folding down into an armchair in a graceful sprawl that signified a level of relaxation that could only make her envious.

Gaby sighed and attempted to mirror his laid-back vibe. 'My first couple of placements were great and I got to travel and use my linguistic abilities. That's what gets me the best jobs—keen parents who want bilingual children or tutoring.'

Angel angled his darkly handsome head to one side. 'Yet I hear a jaded note in your voice.'

Gaby grimaced. 'Because my last two jobs were *too* challenging. First, I landed an employer who wanted to turn me into a maid of all work round the clock to justify my excellent salary.'

'Were you living in the household?' Angel queried.

'I usually do.'

'That makes you an easy target.'

Gaby winced and gazed down into her wine glass. 'My duties are listed on my employment contract, but I had to resign to enforce them and, as always, I hated leaving the kids because I had become attached to them. It was the job I took after that one, though, that was the *real* problem…'

The silence hummed. Angel studied her, admiring the copper shine of her hair in the lamplight, the pale perfection of her dainty profile, the long feathery lashes momentarily veiling the dark blue depths of her eyes.

'And the problem *was*…?' Angel prompted, watching as she glanced up through her lashes and bit at her full pink lower lip, sending a roar of arousal coursing through him that tightened every defensive muscle in his lean, hard body.

Gaby tensed. 'The husband. The wife and the children were lovely but he…he was scary.'

Angel stiffened and sat forward, brilliant dark golden eyes now intent. 'How…scary?'

'He was a banker. He asked me to join him for a drink once when his wife was abroad and I said no and he didn't make anything of it, but he began to hang around when I was looking after his kids…and of course I couldn't object to that,' she pointed out ruefully. 'I was careful to act very much like an employee to keep the boundaries up. Unfortunately, it didn't stop him. There were little admiring remarks, little touches, never anything I could make a fuss about though, and he would stand too close, getting right into my space. It was intimidating. He was a big guy.'

Becoming increasingly restless as he listened, Angel sprang upright, his anger stirred by the thought of her being frightened by another man. 'And *then*?'

'My room was in the basement and he began to come down there at night and walk up and down the corridor. I went out once and he said he was reorganising the wine cellar, and maybe he was, but it went on for weeks. It got to the stage that every time I looked up, he was close by, watching me. I got nervous and tried to avoid him, but it was hopeless. I felt like I was being stalked. I was scared of him, scared of what he might try to do if he got the opportunity,' she admitted, her eyes stinging with guilty tears.

'Of course you were scared.' Angel sank down on the sofa beside her, startling her, and she lifted her head to look at him. 'Any woman would have felt threatened by that kind of behaviour…and presumably there were times when you were alone in the house with him?'

'Yes,' Gaby conceded, relieved by his understanding and grateful for it as well because it was not a story she had shared with anyone else, fearful that they might suspect she had been flirtatious and had somehow invited the man's unwelcome interest. 'And I hated those times when his wife was away. I went out those evenings if I could…but then he would be hanging around when I came back, acting creepily friendly.'

Angel appraised her pale, anxious face and the teardrop inching its way down over a delicate cheekbone and something cracked inside him, unleashing a tangled flood of emotions that powered right through and straight past his innate reserve and distrust of women. It was a gut response to curve a supportive arm around her taut, trembling spine. 'Why on earth are you crying and sounding so apologetic about what must have been a ghastly experience?'

Setting her glass down, Gaby sucked in a shuddering breath and coiled helplessly into the comforting heat of him. 'The whole thing made me feel so weak and I didn't feel safe, yet all the time I was worrying that maybe I was being silly, too imaginative and making a fuss about nothing...or that at some stage, without even realising it, I might have done or said something that encouraged him.'

Angel frowned, his censorious golden eyes in a direct collision with her strained gaze. 'No, you didn't. I know you. You're blameless in this. It was your job to keep yourself safe and he was a threat. He was probably getting off on your fear. It was a power trip for him and sooner or later I believe he would have assaulted you,' he forecast.

Gaby shivered. 'I thought that too. I hated myself for giving way, but I was so scared of him I handed in my notice and warned the agency about him. Unfortunately it's put me off taking another live-in position.'

'Of course it has. Is that why you're here in Alharia in a temporary job that you are vastly overqualified for?'

'Yes...and I needed a breathing space before I decided what to do next.'

'You have to be the least weak woman I have ever met,' Angel intoned in a fierce undertone.

And her tummy flipped an entire somersault in receipt of the glow of appreciation in his stunning gaze. She felt warm, reassured, championed for the first time in her adult life. She had never had anyone behind her before. When she had been bullied at boarding school, her aunt had told her that it was her own fault for winning prizes every year and that being less of a 'brainbox' would make her more friends.

'I never thought that you would admire strength in a woman,' Gaby confided, looking up at him without bothering to hide her surprise.

'I'm no saint…and I *didn't* admire it when you were using that strength of will against me,' Angel told her bluntly.

A helpless gurgle of laughter was wrenched from Gaby at that admission. Sometimes Angel was so honest that he made her toes curl. Embarrassed by an amusement that struck her as less than generous, she buried her hot face in his jacket. If she was as honest with herself, that strength of hers five years ago had only been staged for his benefit and her pride. Never had she wanted so badly to have an excuse to give in and settle for a casual fling with a man who only wanted her body and nothing else from her. But Angel hadn't given her that excuse because he didn't lie, and he didn't pretend. He had been quite upfront about his desire only for sex. The recollection still pained her and in response she pushed her troubled face harder into his lean, muscular shoulder.

The warm, achingly familiar scent of him engulfed her in an intoxicating wave. He smelt good enough to eat. There was a hint of his usual cologne with an undertone of clean, spicy masculinity that made her nipples tighten and her thighs press together. That fast, that naturally, her body reacted to Angel with the off-the-charts sizzling chemistry that had almost destroyed her the last time they were together. That craving had almost torn her apart. Shaken by the surge of reaction gripping her, Gaby lifted her head and tried to will herself into backing away.

'You're a snuggler,' Angel condemned, his extraordinary dark golden eyes locked to her flushed face.

'Guilty as charged,' Gaby conceded.

His dark head angled down, and she literally stopped breathing. He looked as though he were on the brink of kissing her and she wanted him to kiss her so badly but, if it hadn't happened five years ago, what were the chances of it happening now? Back then Angel had thought far in advance of his every move, foreseeing every possible betrayal and complication in his relationships. He had wanted the reassurance of a signed non-disclosure agreement before he became intimate with a woman. And Gaby had *refused* to sign and that had been that, the end of the road before she even got walking down it, because Angel would not take the risk of trusting her to that extent.

'You smell of…roses, is it?' Angel murmured, staring down at her, dark eyes glowing, gleaming gold, exotically fringed by a luxuriant ring of dense black curling lashes. His tawny eyes were so gorgeous it was hard to look away from him.

'Yes…er…fancy skincare creams in my en suite,' Gaby mumbled, and it was as if time was slowing down for her as the tension between them thrummed like a warning drumbeat. 'We shouldn't be this close.'

'If you were a fire, no matter how many warnings I was given I would still get burned. It was always like that,' Angel told her sibilantly, his breath ghosting across her cheek as he brought his lips down to the level of hers and kissed her.

His acknowledgement that he still wanted her as much as he had years earlier lifted Gaby's self-esteem to giddy heights and made her feel more secure. What she was feeling was *not* one-sided; it was mutual. His mouth on hers wasn't just a kiss, though, or indeed anything like any kiss she had had before. Her hands travelled up slowly over his broad chest to his strong shoulders and into his hair, because a kiss from Angel shot her onto another plane entirely.

Her fingertips toyed with the thick black silky hair at his nape, shaping the base of his skull. His tongue traced the seam of her lips and then delved between, ignited a lightning storm inside her that sent sensual sensation arrowing along every nerve ending she possessed. A violent shiver rattled through her, a piercing sweetness rising as his tongue duelled with her own. It was electrifying as her nipples swelled and pinched taut and she pressed instinctively closer to him, squirming as a pool of liquid heat gathered in her pelvis.

'That was worth waiting for,' she gasped inanely as he released her lips to drag in a shuddering breath.

Laughter rippled through Angel as he stared down into her flushed face, revelling in the blueness of her eyes. 'I don't want to stop…' he confessed in a driven undertone.

'I'm not signing anything!' Gaby exclaimed as though he had flipped a switch on her, and as more colour flooded her anxious face at that embarrassing exclamation she reached up a hand and gently framed a high sculpted cheekbone. 'Can't you trust me that far?'

'I don't carry round non-disclosure agreements in my back pocket,' Angel countered with sardonic bite. 'And there's no personal insult in the provisions I take to protect myself. I have never fully trusted any woman.'

'I think that's sad,' Gaby told him truthfully while at the same time a tiny bit of panic was gripping her, because she had just given him the green light to go ahead without even properly thinking about what she was doing.

Yet choosing to be with Angel felt seductively like following a natural instinct and surrendering to the inevitable. Fighting the desire to be with him five years earlier had been a serious challenge. Back then she had still suffered from the illusion that Mr Perfect was probably waiting to meet her round the next corner in her life and she had been content to have faith and wait, had naively assumed that some day soon another man would make her feel exactly what Angel made her feel.

Only it hadn't happened, and, goodness knew, she had tried hard to recapture that sizzling connection with someone else. In Angel's wake, however, real life had proved a downer. She had met men who groped, men who demanded, even men who made passes at her friends. Indeed, she had met every combination of bad in the male sex and several men who were perfectly decent and acceptable but not one of whom had inspired the insane craving that Angel could incite with one wickedly sensual smile. It had taught her a lesson. It had taught her to look back with regret at the experience she had missed out on, although she had never regretted refusing to sign that non-disclosure agreement. That had been a line she refused to cross even for his benefit.

'Maybe it is sad but that's how it is for me,' Angel parried without apology, swooping down to capture her mouth again. 'Am I moving too fast for you? I plead guilty... I am insanely impatient, and the first time there'll probably be more speed and passion than finesse, but I promise to make it up to you the next time...'

He was so outspoken that Gaby didn't know where to look. She had never been open about sex. She had had to fake knowledge she didn't have to fit in when she was younger but as she'd matured she had simply sought friends who slept around less and didn't judge her for her more old-fashioned outlook.

Gaby trembled as his lips caressed hers, every sense on a high of exhilaration at the taste and the scent and the feel of him against her. The strap of her dress loosened and slid off her shoulder and she tensed, gasping into his mouth as he unbuttoned its twin.

'Time we moved this to a more private place,' Angel told her, springing upright and bending down to lift her clean off the sofa before she had even guessed what he was planning to do.

He carried her into the bedroom next door and settled her down on a huge ornately carved wooden bed in a far grander room than the one she had been allotted. It reminded her of the differences between them, the fact that she was staff and that he was usually the boss in every scenario. Only not *her* boss, she reminded herself as she lay back, striving to seem calm, only she wasn't calm with her brain running riot. She didn't want him to know that he would be her first lover. Angel would see significance in that and possibly even think she was a little bit weird for still being so inexperienced at her age. No way was she willing to give him that satisfaction!

Angel shed his jacket, his tie and kicked off his shoes with a haste that was unlike him. He stared at the woman on the bed, the embodiment and fulfilment of a dream and a long-held fantasy, he conceded abstractedly.

Possibly there was some excuse for that uncool haste of his. She looked amazing, her hair tumbling across the pillow in a silken cloud of colourful waves, blue eyes with the depth of gemstones luminous against her porcelain skin.

He unbuttoned his shirt, unzipped his trousers, the eager throb at his groin growing in intensity as she watched him.

As his lean bronzed physique emerged from his discarded clothing, Gaby was mesmerised. He was all hard contours and strength, from the ripple of muscles across his abdomen as he moved to the breadth of his hair-roughened chest. A dark furrow of hair dissected his flat stomach and ran down out of sight into his boxers and there her gaze lingered, warmth blooming in her cheeks because the fine fabric accentuated his jutting arousal.

He dropped down on the bed beside her, lifting her up and reaching for her unstrapped dress to slide it up over her head. As her breasts were bared Angel expelled his breath in a rush. 'Beautiful,' he husked, his hands rising to cup the full swells, his thumbs grazing across the swollen nipples, making her shiver because she was incredibly sensitive there. He lowered her down to the pillows again and whisked off her last garment without her even properly being aware of it.

Shifting against her lazily, he angled back his hips to remove the boxers, and for several heart-stopping seconds as he came back to her she felt him rubbing against her lower stomach, and then he rose up on his elbows and crushed her parted lips hungrily beneath his again, rolling her over and stroking her breasts. He trailed his mouth down the slope of her shoulder and caught a straining nipple between his fingers, closing his lips round the swollen tip and tugging on it. A tiny moan escaped her, her hips rising at the ache forming between her legs.

Kneading the soft swells, he utilised the edge of his teeth and flicked his tongue across the rosy buds, creating a chain reaction to the heart of her that made her clench her inner muscles tight. When he directed his attention to her damp core and circled her clitoris, it was too much stimulation for her overexcited body and a climax engulfed her at shattering speed. Her body convulsing, she was insensible to everything for some moments and then she blinked up at him in surprise and faint mortification as though that lack of control had shamed her.

'I like that you're as ready for this as I am,'

Angel growled appreciatively, shifting down the bed, long fingers trailing down a still-trembling thigh.

And Gaby closed her eyes tight as he parted her legs because she had always wondered about *that* practice and she wasn't going to let shyness and embarrassment come between her and the chance of enjoyment. He ran his tongue over her tender core and, from that first teasing caress, she was electrified, reduced to a quivering bundle of thrumming impatience and anticipation, so intense she could barely dwell on the pleasure because her body was screaming for the finishing line. And when it came in a flood of convulsive blistering pleasure she cried out in wonder because she had never felt anything that powerful before, and in the aftermath she felt boneless.

But Angel didn't allow her to rest back and relax, he gathered her up again and ravished her swollen mouth with his own, his lean, powerful body hard and hungry against her as they strained together and she felt him glide between her legs, both smooth and something slightly colder and more abrasive brushing against her. *Cold?* A faint furrow of confusion indented her brow as his movements ensured he partially entered her wet channel and her every sense screamed with anticipation.

'I should have a condom on,' Angel breathed, and he abruptly withdrew from her again, pulling back from her to reach for protection.

It was only once he leant back to deftly don a contraceptive that she realised that he was pierced, and before she had even thought about it she was reaching out to brush a fingertip over one of the steel beads that had touched her. 'I wondered; I didn't realise—'

'It's called a Jacob's Ladder. I had it done when I was eighteen and aching to be the coolest kid ever. It hurt like hell, and took for ever to heal, but women like it and some believe it adds to their pleasure,' he imparted with wry amusement.

Gaby reddened, out of her depth and feeling it at that moment. Angel came back to her, dark golden eyes ablaze with hunger. 'I don't usually spend the whole night with a woman, but I think I'll break that rule for you. Prepare to be ravaged within an inch of your life,' he teased.

'What will the ravaging consist of?'

'As much down-and-dirty sex as we have the energy to enjoy,' Angel asserted with a flashing smile of scorching confidence.

And she envied him. Oh, how she envied

him in that instant for his sheer sexual confidence when she was striving to conceal her inexperience. She was terrified of him noticing that she was a virgin, terrified of doing something that gave that embarrassing little secret away. 'It's been a while for me,' she remarked carefully.

'How long?'

'Months,' she told him tightly without meeting his eyes. 'I've had to move around a lot this year.'

Angel bent down to nibble at her full lower lip while he stroked her quivering body, firing up responses that had momentarily gone into abeyance. A spiralling heat warmed her lower body, desire sparking afresh, blurring her insecurities. 'I imagine you're very choosy,' he murmured huskily. 'I'm lucky to have made the cut.'

Gaby laughed. 'I can't take you being humble seriously.'

'Enjoy it while it lasts, *kardoula mou*,' Angel advised, shifting over her, and settling between her thighs before tipping her up and surging forward.

Gaby buried her face in his shoulder, drinking in the evocative scent of his skin, striving not to tense, not to give way to nerves, not to expose herself in any way. He entered her in one deep thrust and pain and pleasure warred together, her heart rate speeding up until it seemed to be thundering inside her chest. She unclenched her teeth, hoping that that single jolt of pain meant that the worst of her initiation was over. She felt stretched, invaded, alarmingly sensitive as he moved and a strong wave of powerful pleasure traversed her lower body, much more satisfying than she had expected. He plunged deeper still, and elation tugged at her, backed by a renewed need that clawed at her with the most wicked impatience.

Feverish excitement claimed her, and she arched up to him, writhing in pleasure as he moved faster and harder, her lips parting on a moan of mingled delight and surprise. Feeling freed from her physical self, she surrendered to the hot drowning pleasure pounding through her. Release came in a great wave of sensation and he loosed an uninhibited shout of satisfaction as he reached the same conclusion.

Gaby blinked back the strangest moisture flooding her eyes. It had been *that* good that it had knocked her emotionally off balance, she told herself uneasily. Well, hadn't she chosen well when she decided that she would go ahead and take a chance on him? But enough was enough. If he didn't usually spend the whole night with a woman, she wasn't going to be the woman who urged him to break his rules.

'I should go back to my own room,' she whispered shakily.

An offer that would usually have relieved Angel only made him tighten his hold on her. 'I want you to stay. Let's make the most of being together here.'

And Gaby thought about it and reckoned that it could probably seem a bit nervy on her part to flee the instant the deed had been done. She knew that what he was really saying was that she would never see him again, that their intimacy was a one-off event and not to be repeated. Well, she wasn't naive enough to have expected any other denouement. From what she knew of his reputation, 'one and done', as she had once heard a guy quip, was Angel's normal modus operandi.

'Gabriella...' he pressed in the silence.

'I'm thinking about it. I think it would be better if I left now.'

'Only if you take me with you for the rest of the night.'

Gaby laughed at that idea. 'I only have a single bed and a little slot of a room. It wouldn't be quite your style.'

'Let's stay where we're comfortable, then…
you were spectacular, *glykia mou*. I can't let
you go yet.'

He hadn't noticed that he was her first, Gaby
savoured, relaxing a little on that thought. Not
losing face with Angel was of paramount im-
portance to her. He slid out of bed and strode
into the adjoining bathroom. Light framed his
tousled black hair and tall powerful back view
and not a smidgeon of regret assailed her.

It was perfect, she told herself happily.
There were no witnesses, no cameras, nobody at all to remark on their brief intimacy.
It was casual and private. By the time morning came, she supposed it would get a little
awkward, but her flight was mid-morning.

'I can't afford to sleep in,' she warned him.

'I won't let you. I routinely wake up at
dawn,' Angel murmured, sliding into the bed
beside her again and pulling her inexorably
back to him.

Standing at the foot of the bed in the dawn
light filtering through the curtains, Angel
viewed the sleeping woman. Copper hair as
vibrant as Gabriella was in spirit spilled across
the pillow, a delicate flush on her cheeks, a
peaceful curve to her intoxicating pink lips.

The night had been unforgettable…but now it was over.

Angel didn't do complicated with women and anything with Gabriella was destined to get messy. Without a signed NDA, he had taken a major risk with her, choosing to trust her this *one* time. Now he needed to walk away. He *had* to walk away. Intelligence told him that he had no alternative because he would not have a future with any woman until he took a wife. Gabriella was under his skin but, unlike his weak father, he was *not* in thrall to Gabriella, and he was strong enough to walk away. He would leave Gabriella a note. His private phone number? He winced and decided that encouraging any kind of ongoing contact with a woman who contravened his rules would be inadvisable. So what if she labelled him a four-letter word of a guy? He would never see her again—*never, ever,* he swore to himself grimly.

CHAPTER THREE

'YOU HAVE OPTIONS,' Gaby's friend Liz reminded Gaby ruefully, several weeks after
that night in Alharia.

Gaby grimaced. Yes, she knew the options.
There was termination and there was adop-
tion, both of which were terrifyingly final.
She couldn't face either choice and, in fact,
that part of her that had long dreamt of having a family again actually wanted to *celebrate* the pleasure of becoming a mother.
Stark terror, however, threatened to drown
that guilty seedling of joy. The prospect of
single parenthood was decidedly scary. Somehow, she would manage, she told herself urgently, although she suspected that her job
as a nanny would become too physically demanding when she reached late pregnancy.
She would have to find less taxing work by
that stage, and she didn't have much time

left because she was already more than three months along.

How had the unthinkable happened? That one night in Alharia still haunted her. She would never forget waking up alone in that palace bedroom, feeling very much like a meaningless one-night stand. A servant had wakened her with breakfast in bed. Presumably, Angel had organised that before his slick and silent departure. Gaby had felt too sick with angry mortification to eat and had fled back to her own room to pack. Angel hadn't even left her his phone number. No matter what lens she used to look back on that night, her perspective didn't change: Angel had treated her like dirt, disposable dirt. The least he could have done was wake her to say goodbye before he left but, instead, he had settled for the easier option.

'If you're planning to keep the baby, you'll need the father's support to make that possible,' Liz pointed out sensibly. 'It's hard and very expensive to raise a child alone.'

Gaby gritted her teeth at the concept of Angel being supportive in such circumstances. He would do what the law demanded for a child he didn't want but she was quite certain that he would not wish to be an active parent. He would be angry, bitter and hostile and there was nothing she could do to change that reality. As a man who proudly conserved his royal dignity, determined not to even have his name linked with a woman's in the press, he would scarcely welcome an illegitimate child.

'I'll tell him in a few months' time,' she remarked stiffly.

'You shouldn't leave it that long,' her friend contended. 'Give him time to adjust to the idea before the birth.'

Gaby shrugged. She knew what she had to do but she was in no hurry to do it. 'I could have a miscarriage…or something, so I should wait. And if I leave telling him a bit longer, there'll be no room for him to suggest a termination.'

Liz frowned. 'Would he do that?'

'I really don't know but I'm not willing to put myself in that position,' Gaby admitted quietly. 'It'll be enough if he knows before the baby is born.'

'I still can't believe you had the bad luck to run into Angel Diamandis abroad where you'd be all alone with him,' the blonde lamented. 'I mean, what were the odds that you would meet your first love again like that?'

Gaby wrinkled her nose. 'He wasn't my first love, well, not in the way you mean.'

'Gaby, you were besotted with him, and Laurie and I hated him because he was such a player and he *knew* what he was doing to you when he demanded that stupid agreement from you! You would've got badly hurt if you had got any closer to him,' Liz said feelingly. 'And now look what's happened!'

'I'm a big girl and I got tempted. I didn't expect *this* development.' Gaby sighed, reflecting that Angel had used contraception throughout the night, although he had possibly been a little careless in not taking precautions sooner the first time. 'If I'd been on contraception myself, I suppose I would have been safe from this happening…but I swear Angel is the only man alive who could make me behave the way I did.'

'You and how many other women? Yes, he's incredibly hot, but he is also very much a bad boy and dangerous.' Liz groaned, vaulting upright as a baby's cry sounded upstairs in the small terraced house. 'I'd better get Robbie, and don't forget that he arrived even though George and I were *careful*. Only abstinence is a foolproof method of birth control.'

Chastened by the reminder, Gaby thought about the baby she had conceived. She had seen her child on the ultrasound screen and that viewing had stolen her heart at first glance, wiping out every sensible thought.

But her pregnancy had still come as a huge surprise. Her menstrual cycle had not stopped completely until the second month and she had been so busy working short-term placements and finding a flat share that she hadn't noticed. Her breasts had got bigger, but she had simply thought she was putting on weight. Only the final cessation of her cycle had warned her that something was wrong. Liz and her sister, Laurie, had been stunned when she had finally told them about her night with Angel in Alharia, and although her friends had then persuaded her to do a pregnancy test, she had still been genuinely shocked by the result.

Even so, she refused to let herself panic. In due course, she would make a discreet approach to Angel, although she was in no hurry to do so. After all, he had made his lack of interest in her clear by not contacting her again. Had he wished to seek her out he could've easily discovered where she worked, but he clearly had not wished to see her again. And that was fine. A one-night stand didn't make a relationship, only it was more than a little disheartening to appreciate that a guy who had once flooded her flat with flowers to impress her had walked away from their night of passion with such ease, consigning their brief intimacy to history.

Her thoughts pulled her back into the past and she remembered how Angel had ferried her back to his elegant Cambridge town house after she fell down the steps in front of him. He had put plasters on her cut knees, making her feel like a child again. His friends had sat around being polite but staring, visibly unable to comprehend his interest in her. Inevitably, Angel had been part of the student elite, beautifully dressed and wealthy young people, several who also enjoyed titles or famous parents and who, even though they attended the same university, lived an entirely different and more glamorous life than more ordinary students.

Gaby had been mesmerised by those dark golden eyes fringed by inky black lashes. Breathing that close to Angel had been a challenge and when he had asked her out to dinner, she had loosed an uncomfortable laugh and had said that she was too busy studying to go out in the evenings. Realising that he was a prince, as everyone else treated him with near reverence, had turned her off rather than *on* and his surprise at her rejection had embarrassed her even more.

'I'll change your mind,' he had told her confidently and that afternoon the flowers had arrived, ridiculously extravagant, gorgeous baskets overflowing with exotic blooms that had so cluttered her small living space that she'd had to give most of them away to neighbours and friends.

Naively, she had associated the giving of flowers with romance. The next time she had run into Angel had been at the library. Over coffee she had thanked him for the flowers, and she had been ready to say yes to dinner should he have asked her again, only Angel had told her instead that he was flying home for three weeks. Regrettably, his disappearance had only fuelled her infatuation.

'Angel plays with girls like you, that's all. Don't start building fantasy castles in the air just because he's interested in you at the moment…a moment is as long as Angel's interest lasts,' Cassia Romano had told her bitchily, going out of her way to *bump* into Gaby after a lecture and deliver that unnecessary warning.

Cassia, a blonde with the looks of a supermodel and reputedly the holder of a defunct Italian aristocratic title, had never strayed far from Angel's side. He had treated Cassia like a friend, but Gaby had recognised that possessive Cassia was ambitious to be rather more than that.

Gaby had run into Angel his first day back in the UK and had agreed to dine out with him that evening with her emotions running on high.

'We've got absolutely nothing in common,' she had told him uneasily.

'What does that matter?' Angel had asked lazily. 'We only get one chance to make the most of being young and single. I'm not ashamed to admit that I'm not in the market for anything more serious.'

And that candour of his had acted on her that night like the warning jolt of lightning, blowing her romantic hopes sky-high with the truth that Angel, the ruling Prince of Themos, did not see their relationship progressing beyond the level of a fling. She should have backed off then, she reflected, five years older and wiser, but in those days she had been very much into excusing or glamorising Angel's every flaw. She had told herself that his honesty was refreshing and that she should not condemn him for it. After all, she was still a teenager and wasn't looking to settle down either. And that night she had decided that he would become her first lover. Never in her life had she even imagined the sheer strength of the physical attraction that Angel exuded for her.

'You'll only be another notch on his bed-post,' her friends had warned her.

'But he'll be the first notch on mine,' Gaby had parried, lifting her chin.

'That's not enough when you're already obsessed with him. You'll want more.'

But Gaby had already known that 'more' was not on offer and rather than walk away from a fling that refused to be a fantasy at that stage she had decided that she would settle for what she could get. Only it hadn't turned out like that because, after a couple of more casual meetings, when Angel still studiously refrained from touching her in any way, she had asked him why that was so. And he had explained that he didn't risk getting involved or being alone with a woman unless she had signed a non-disclosure agreement promising never to take photos or talk about him to anybody. He had presented the concept as being protective for both of them because it would have barred him from ever discussing her with anyone either. But the idea of signing a legal agreement to get any closer to Angel had chilled Gaby to the marrow as well as insulted her integrity.

For a start she hadn't liked it being almost

taken for granted that they would become lovers when whether she would or not was for her to decide in the moment. She had been repulsed by his lack of trust in her sex and disturbed that he didn't already realise that she wasn't a social climber, a gold-digger or a woman keen to attract publicity. She had told him that she couldn't possibly sign such a document. He had done his own case no favours when he'd pointed out that every other woman he had been with in recent years had agreed to the measure. He had, admittedly, endeavoured to explain himself and had assured her that he would ensure that she had her own legal advice, but it had all been too much and simultaneously too *little* for Gaby when set beside her own foolish romantic hopes.

She had had a mini meltdown and had told him that she would never sign the document and that they were done. Angel had come over all blue-blooded royalty and had reacted with icy dignity, a response that had given her wounded feelings absolutely no satisfaction. Her only consolation in the final row that had followed the day afterwards was that Angel had lost his temper as well.

The next evening, her friends had accused her of moping and had dragged her out to a party. Angel had been there. He had acknowledged her with a casual inclination of his handsome dark head but had made no attempt to speak to her. An hour later she had seen him kiss another woman out on the terrace, a woman she had seen him with before, and shock and possessive rage had assailed her. While she had told herself that it was over between them, in the back of her mind she had expected him to return to her. When he had reappeared back inside, she had breezed past him and hissed in an undertone that he was a dirty, rotten cheater.

Enraged by that condemnation, Angel had called at the flat she had shared with the twins an hour later.

'We are over. You don't own me,' he had told her.

And she had flung a teddy bear at him, the only thing within reach. Mortification still seized her whenever she remembered that moment.

Angel, however, had reacted as seriously as though she had thrown a brick at him. 'You refused to sign an NDA,' he had reminded her doggedly.

'What sort of a man in today's world asks a woman to sign an NDA?' she had slammed back at him, punctuating her demand with a rather more solid pottery mug.

Angel had ducked and the window behind him had been smashed and as shards of glass went flying in all directions he had closed a hand round her arm and furiously demanded, 'Are you crazy?' His tawny eyes had blazed gold as the heart of a fire.

Shaken by the damage she had caused and embarrassed when her friends came rushing in to check on them, she had backed away. 'I'm not saying sorry,' she had told him childishly. 'I wish I'd hit you!'

And those had been her very last words to Angel five years earlier. And that was what bothered her most about Angel. The feelings he triggered inside her were too powerful and he made her too needy. It took her back to the savage loss of her family at fourteen when she had first learned how much it hurt to lose anyone you loved. She could neither afford nor wish to develop such feelings for Angel.

Angel studied the email and gritted his teeth. He had been ignoring it in his inbox, reluctant to open it, to be forced to handle the conflicting reactions assailing him at the sight of her name. Only now was he finally reading it, only to be taken aback by its very brevity.

I need to meet with you in person concerning an urgent personal matter.

He was conscious of a savage sense of disappointment. He really had believed in his heart of hearts that Gabriella Knox differed from his previous lovers, but that she should contact him months after their Alharian encounter was revealing, he reflected with angry scepticism. Obviously, she wanted something from him, as so many of her predecessors had, and his wide experience of such approaches suggested that what she wanted was most probably money. Or another night with him?

That would have been Angel's preferred option, but even that was controversial because he knew he could not afford to surrender to temptation again. Memories of that night had plagued him ever since and unnerved a man who considered himself stable as a rock in that line. He didn't repeat his sexual encounters, considering it far simpler and safer to simply move on to a fresh conquest. Such recollections didn't usually linger, nor did they have the weird effect of making him ridiculously critical of the other women he met, while just thinking about Gabriella still made him hard. So, no, he definitely didn't want to see *her* again, but innate caution warned him that he had to check out *why* Gabriella had got in touch. And he would guard against any inappropriate further familiarity by bringing legal counsel with him, he decided with a forbidding smile. *That* would impose a barrier and would also ensure that he stuck strictly to business.

Three weeks later, Gaby climbed laboriously off the bus and walked towards the hotel at which Angel had agreed to meet her. So much cloak-and-dagger nonsense, she reflected ruefully. Did he really see that as still necessary? Still, she could concede that, given the choice, he would not want to be seen in public with a pregnant woman lest he was exposed as the father, but, barring anyone looking *very* carefully at her, she had done her very best to conceal her condition.

She wore a voluminous winter coat over a loose black knit sweater dress and long boots. She was more than eight months pregnant and had not intended to leave telling Angel quite so late, but it had taken a month for her to get a response to her email and then another few weeks to set up the appointment and regrettably she had not factored in that time lag. Perhaps she should consider herself lucky that Angel was willing to agree to an actual meeting, she thought irritably, but really approaching the Queen would have been easier than gaining access to the ruling Prince of Themos.

It was only fair that she tell him that she was having a child…a little boy. Angel had a right to know he was soon to become a father. It didn't mean that she was expecting anything from him, she reasoned soothingly, bolstering her proud independence.

'Are you Miss Knox?' A man in a suit with a security bud in his ear approached her the instant she entered the hotel foyer.

Gaby stilled in surprise. 'Yes.'

'Please come this way,' the man urged quietly.

She was swiftly ushered into a lift by the man, much as though she were engaging in espionage, and her mouth quirked, her sense of humour tickled. Certainly, it would be the only thing she had to smile about on this particular day, she reflected unhappily, because she was not looking forward to telling Angel news that he would not want to hear. Angel would not be familiar with being put in that invidious position, particularly when he had no control over the situation. One of the first things she had noticed about Angel was that he liked and even expected to control everything happening around and to him. He fervently guarded himself from the unexpected. And what could be more unexpected and unwelcome than an unplanned pregnancy?

Pale at that knowledge, Gaby accompanied the security man out of the lift and straight to the door, which opened ahead of them. An unfamiliar brunette in her thirties appeared in the doorway and gave her a frosty appraisal. 'Miss Knox? Gabriella Knox?' she queried.

'Who's asking?' Gaby countered quietly.

'I'm here, Gabriella,' Angel's dark deep drawl sounded from deeper in the room, cold and audibly edged with impatience.

Gaby crossed the threshold, conscious of the woman closing the door behind her and remaining with them. 'I didn't realise that I would have to ask to see you alone,' she said flatly.

'This is one of my lawyers, Petronella Casey,' Angel informed her calmly.

Gaby lifted her head high and squared her shoulders. 'I'm not prepared to talk to you with a third party present,' she told him, scanning him with veiled eyes, taking in the superbly tailored grey designer suit, the wine-red shirt, a gold playing card cufflink visible at one wrist. Tall, dark, breathtakingly handsome and sophisticated, but still flawed and imperfect when he could greet a brief email with such cynical distrust and distaste.

She marvelled that he could still look so beautiful and yet act as remote as the Andes from her, as if that night in Alharia had never happened, as if she were an absolute stranger. It hurt, of course it did, but she rammed that hurt down deep inside her and strove to rise above it, trying not to dwell on the lowering awareness that any kind of involvement with Angel had always caused her pain. It was a little too late to be reminding herself now of that sobering reality, she conceded wretchedly.

The brunette stepped forward. 'I assure you that whatever is said in this room will remain completely confidential,' she declared, with a cool smile that might have been intended as reassuring but which missed its mark when she had 'legal shark' written all over her.

Gaby had no intention of being humiliated by the presence of another woman in the room while she staged a deeply personal and private conversation with Angel. 'I'm afraid it's a question of you leaving…or *me* leaving,' she explained with quiet dignity.

'Be reasonable, Gabriella,' Angel intoned in the most forbidding tone she had ever heard from him.

Angel studied her in frustration, absently

wondering if she had come direct from a funeral, because the long all-black outfit seemed like overkill otherwise and, what was worse, swallowed her tiny stature alive, literally covering her from head to toe. But simultaneously the colour black also threw the splendour of her shining copper hair, dark blue eyes and faultless porcelain skin into prominence, lending her the luminous quality of a star against the night sky, a poetic thought so unlike his usual thought processes that Angel almost winced for himself.

'Why should I be reasonable when you're being so unreasonable?' Gaby asked sharply, flinching as her baby boy tumbled inside her and kicked hard against her bladder. He was a very active baby and a large one. A date for her C-section delivery was already set. 'I came here to speak to you in private but if you can't even grant me that courtesy, I'll leave.'

The lawyer, Petronella, stepped forward without warning. 'If you're in agreement, I'll wait outside, sir. You can call me back in at any stage.'

Colliding with Petronella's intent gaze, Gaby reddened as she grasped that the lawyer had recognised the reason behind her desire for privacy. Of course, another woman *would* notice that she had dressed to hide her body faster than the average man and have worked out why.

Angel shifted a hand in a gesture of agreement but settled angry dark golden eyes on Gaby. Such stunning eyes, she thought with regret at the prospect of what was coming, tawny brown with the glow of honey in sunlight and ringed by lush black spiky lashes.

As the door snapped shut on the lawyer's exit, Angel stared at her. 'Right…just get to the point quickly and we'll wrap this up,' he urged harshly.

'What did I ever do to you to deserve such a lack of good manners?' Gaby asked in helpless condemnation.

A faint rise of red over his high cheekbones told her that she had made a direct hit and the bad side of Gaby rejoiced while the more sensible side of her winced, because riling Angel was scarcely in her best interests in her current predicament.

'I apologise if I've been curt,' Angel breathed between gritted teeth. 'But it has been many months since our last meeting in Alharia and naturally I am curious as to why you have demanded this meeting.'

'It wasn't a demand, Angel. I believe it was a polite request,' Gaby protested, struggling to keep her hot temper under control. 'But since you urged me to get to the point, I'll do that and free us both from this unpleasant confrontation.'

'It is *not* a confrontation!' Angel bit back at her in a seriously rattled undertone.

'Oh, I think it *is* when you greet me with a lawyer by your side,' Gaby contradicted with confidence, an icy flash lightening her blue eyes. 'Relax, Angel. I'm only here as a courtesy and I have no intention of approaching the press in any shape or form. However, you do have the right to know that I'm…' she hesitated '…pregnant.'

And the word fell like a giant rock dropped into a still pond. That imaginary resounding splash was as loud as the shattering silence.

Later she thought that she would never, as long as she lived, forget the look of pure naked antipathy and contempt that flared in Angel's lean, hard-boned features as he intoned very drily, 'Well, if you *are*, it can't possibly be mine!'

CHAPTER FOUR

STATED RIGHT UP FRONT, before she even got the chance to speak in her own defence, Angel's explicit rebuttal was a daunting challenge.

'You seem very sure of that,' Gaby responded without any expression at all, although her small figure was stiff and her face pale. His icy expression and the rigid tension spliced into his lean powerful frame were totally unfamiliar to her. It was as if something had flipped in Angel, something she hadn't met with in him before.

'I am. Have you any idea how often I've been through this scenario with other women?' Angel derided with a curled lip. '*Four* times at the last count! I know exactly what happens next. You will threaten me with legal action and take it to court for a DNA test and only then will your claim be exposed for the lie that it is. As I'm sure you know you can make a great deal of money out of the publicity that any paternity case against me will give you.'

'I've already told you that I don't want publicity and the only claim I would make would be support for our child.'

'Don't say "our"!' Angel incised. 'It's offensive! If you are carrying a child, it is *not mine.*'

Gaby breathed in slow and deep, tamping down her ire with difficulty. But, if Angel had already been falsely accused on several occasions of having fathered a child, she could at least understand his distrust even if she resented it. 'I am not those other women, Angel,' she began. 'And—'

'But you've just proved that you *are* by forcing me to meet up with you and trying to pass off some other man's child as mine!' Angel condemned, nostrils flared on his classic straight nose, his strong masculine jaw at an aggressive angle. His eyes shimmered gold, narrowed, dagger-sharp and angry.

'Why are you so convinced that this is not your child? Aside from your outrage that I should *dare* to confront you with this development, please explain,' Gaby urged thinly. 'Are you infertile? Specially blessed not to reproduce by your throne? There is no such thing as one hundred per cent efficiency with any form of contraception!'

'But it's remarkable how often it *allegedly* fails for me,' Angel intoned very drily.

'Let me get this straight…you think that you have the right to insult and punish me for your experiences with other women, who lied and plotted to try and entrap you or make money out of their connection with you?' Gaby slammed back at him wrathfully. 'How fair is that?'

'You forced me into this meeting,' Angel derided, his stunning eyes awash with anger. 'What else am I supposed to think?'

Gaby inclined her chin. 'I didn't force anything. I asked politely,' she reminded him curtly. 'This child is *your* child. Nor am I apologising for that when you must know as well as I do that no contraceptive method is totally safe. Let's at least behave like adults here.'

'I am dealing with this like an adult,' Angel sliced in icily.

'No, you're not. You're *ignoring* the situation by making the assumption that I'm lying,' Gaby censured. 'But, in only a few weeks I will give birth to your son.'

'At which time you will doubtless contact a lawyer and make a legal claim, which will eventually go to court and a DNA test,' Angel cut in drily. 'Why would I waste my energy on the issue now?'

When he put it like that, Gaby could see his point when he was so utterly convinced that the child she carried could not possibly be *his* child. Even so, she loathed him for his attitude and knew she would never forgive him for it or for treating her like a con woman, meeting with him to scam and fleece him. 'Well, I've done my duty by informing you of the situation and, considering your mindset, I have absolutely nothing more to say to you. Have a nice life, Angel. You'd have to be dying in a ditch for me to cross your path again!'

With that proud declamation, Gaby stalked out of the room with her head held high and moved back to the lift. When Petronella Casey walked back into the hotel suite, Angel was preoccupied with his thoughts, his lean, darkly handsome features shuttered. He was recalling his mother's infidelity and his father's weak inability to deal with her behaviour. Angel had vowed that he would never allow himself to be put in such a position, and as time had moved on, and he'd learned for himself how dishonest and untrustworthy women could be, his attitudes had only hardened.

'Evidently you do not believe a word that

that young woman said,' Petronella remarked quietly. 'Whereas I suspect that it might be wise to pay a little more attention to her.'

'Of course Gabriella's lying,' Angel asserted with ringing confidence, doubt or insecurity rarely featuring in his decisive nature. But it was also only now occurring to Angel in that same moment that, if she was *not* lying, he had burned his boats with a vengeance. 'She has to be lying, just like her predecessors. Hire a private investigation agency to look into her. I should take every precaution.'

'Bear in mind that in spite of the barrage of paternity claims that you have endured,' Petronella murmured in a diplomatic undertone, 'sooner or later and by the law of averages there will possibly be a woman telling the truth.'

'With respect, I hope you are mistaken,' Angel breathed tautly. 'The first male child born to me is automatically the heir to the throne. That is in our constitution and not something I can change.'

But the question had been raised and he could not ignore it, even if the prospect shot naked alarm through him. What if he were to become a father? How the hell could he ever handle that? He was the product of no parenting, who only knew what to avoid rather than what a father should do.

Gaby walked back into Liz's home with tears walled up in a dam behind her scratchy eyes. She had never been so grateful that her friend was on maternity leave and still accessible rather than back at work. The blonde took one look at Gaby's tight, pale face and immediately gave her a hug. 'It was *that* bad?' she whispered in dismay.

'Yes. Plan A was a major fail, so I will move immediately to plan B,' Gaby quipped a little chokily. 'Angel is not planning to be supportive or involved in any way. He refuses even to recognise that this *could* be his child, so that's that, then.'

'He still has to pay child support, whether he likes it or not,' Liz argued vehemently.

'*If* I can't survive without his help,' Gaby qualified. 'But if I *can* get by, he will never lay eyes again on me or his child in this lifetime.'

Just as Gabriella had spent troubled weeks striving to work out her future with a young child to raise, Angel had, possibly for the very first time in his life, been required to work through months of stress, inconvenience and ultimate disappointment. Why? Gabriella Knox had, to all intents and purposes, disappeared off the face of the earth and, with her, the child Angel now suspected was *his* child as well.

On his monthly trip to London to ensure that the investigation agency he had hired were still making the search for Gabriella a top priority, he learned that there had finally been a breakthrough and intense satisfaction gripped him, the frustration of the past nine months draining away to be replaced by a powerful need for action instead. Now all he had to do was seal the deal and he saw refusal on her part as so unlikely as to be virtually impossible...

Gaby smiled as the early-summer sunshine engulfed her in the garden. It wasn't hot but it was infinitely preferable to another grey wet day. She tossed the clothes pegs and sheets into a basket to carry back indoors. The long winter at the isolated farm had provided a wonderfully therapeutic time out for her, calming wounded and tangled emotions, soothing the painful regrets and showing her the way forward.

And her way forward, she reflected fondly, was definitely through her son, Alexios. She set down the laundry basket for sorting later and padded into the cosy living area, which comprised kitchen, dining and sitting room. An elderly woman sat there in an armchair. Clara Paterson, her friend Liz's godmother, was a widow in her seventies and recovering from recent minor surgery. Clara was currently waiting to move into a more compact property in town and Gaby was staying with her as a temporary housekeeper. Living in the Scottish borders while looking after Clara had given Gaby a comfortable peaceful home while she adjusted to being a new mother.

Not that Alexios, beaming at her from the rug at Clara's feet, looked like much of a challenge, she conceded proudly. He didn't bear much resemblance to her or, for that matter, Angel. Nobody in her family had had bright green eyes or black curls, but then, neither did Angel, so she had no idea whose ancestor had donated those genes. It didn't much matter either, she reflected cheerfully. What *did* matter was that Alexios was a happy, healthy eight-month-old baby, already crawling and trying to talk to her. He had his father's brash confidence and fearless approach to life, but he was infinitely more loving in nature. And Gaby had discovered that not since the death of her family when she was fourteen had she ever loved anyone or anything as much as she loved her baby.

The earth-shattering racket of a helicopter passing overhead barely made her blink because the house was only a few miles from a military base. A frown line pleated her brow, though, when the noise not only failed to recede but also increased and she moved to the front window, disconcerted to see a craft landing in the field beyond the wall surrounding the garden.

Clara peered out of the window beside her. 'That's *not* an army helicopter,' the older woman commented knowledgeably. 'And what's that flag on the bodywork? I don't recognise it...'

But Gaby *did*. The stripes of colour and the dragon logo featured on the flag of Themos. Her slim body froze inside her jeans and sweater, her pale aghast face suddenly washing with colour. 'It's Alexios's father...he's found us.'

'About time too,' Clara remarked calmly. 'You can't hide for ever with a child.'

'But he didn't *want* to know about Alexios!' Gaby protested.

'He's a very stubborn young man but he's had time to see the light. An alpha male can react badly when you plunge him into a situation out of his control,' Clara commented.

'Clara!' Gaby exclaimed in surprise. 'What do you know about alpha males?'

'Probably more than you do,' Clara quipped with a smile. 'I was married to one for almost half a century and there's not a day goes by when I don't miss his bossy, bullheaded ways.'

Gaby patted the old lady's thin hand comfortingly. 'I know…'

'So, go and deal with yours…*sensibly*,' Clara stressed. 'I'll watch Alexios until you're ready to introduce him to his father.'

Gaby was too respectful to tell the older lady just how far removed she was from the point of introducing her son to his very reluctant parent. Instead, she nodded as she watched a tall, frighteningly familiar figure clad in a winter coat and dark suit literally step over the low garden wall and head across the lawn to the rarely used farmhouse front door. She felt sick with stress, but her tummy was twisting with a fury she could not suppress. How dared Angel track her down after the way he had treated her at their last meeting? *How dared he?* There was nothing even slightly sensible about Gaby's attitude to such an incursion into her much-cherished privacy. As the front doorbell wheezed from long disuse, Gaby glimpsed her reflection in the hall mirror, her mass of copper hair tamed and anchored somewhat messily to the back of her head, her flushed face bare of cosmetics. So, she wasn't exactly looking her best and why would she even think about something as trivial as her appearance at such a moment?

Her rage at Angel's characteristic chutz-pah simply boiled over. In the back of her mind were all the times she could have done with the support of her child's father in re-cent months, not least when she had struggled to cope with a newborn's demands just after her C-section or during the many disrupted and sleepless nights that had followed before Alexios had eased into a routine. There had been the rather frightening knowledge that, while friends might help, she was essentially alone and had to handle her own emergencies. Becoming a single parent with that awareness was very stressful and in the early days she had had nightmares about what would happen to Alexios if anything were to happen to her.

Gaby jerked open the front door without unhooking the security chain that allowed it to open only a few inches. Through the gap, though, she saw Angel, with his smoulder-ingly beautiful face that could make angels weep and poets sigh. Silky black hair flopped above his brow and striking tawny eyes set off flawless cheekbones and a full sensual mouth. Once one glance at him had sent wanton shimmers of excitement travelling through her, but this time around seeing Angel was like having an ice cube trail down her rigid spine as she deliberately chose to remember the humiliation he had doled out to her that day in the London hotel.

'I realise that you're probably surprised by my arrival.'

'Gobsmacked!' Gaby shot back at him with deliberate vulgarity.

'May I come in?' Angel dealt her a gleaming narrow-eyed appraisal, the kind of rapier look royalty wore like a blazing shield of confidence, warning her that he was not expecting to meet with any opposition. His audacity only inflamed her more.

'No!' Gaby snapped caustically and she slammed the door shut again. Spinning in a rapid arc, she folded her arms and paced the narrow hall.

Angel pressed the bell again. 'I'm not leaving,' he announced from outside, that perfect diction of his enunciating every syllable with clarity.

Gaby gritted her teeth and only just resisted the childish urge to drag the door open again and scream at him. Nobody could unleash her temper more easily than Angel.

'Is this what you call adult behaviour?' Angel enquired sibilantly from behind the glass door.

Her hands clenched into fierce fists. Had she had a brick in her hand she would have thrown it at him. Instead, she paced up and down the hall, battling to get her tempestuous emotions in check. He was so cool and calm, and it inflamed her when she thought of what he had made *her* endure.

Yet she also knew that what she was feeling wasn't *all* Angel's fault. Time had made her more honest with herself. She had been madly in love with Angel at university and he had hurt her badly. It had not been a girlish infatuation that she could quickly put behind her, it had been full-blown over-the-top love, bordering on obsession. And, sadly for her, some lingering shard of those soft, sappy feelings had made her succumb to that one-night stand in Alharia because the attraction had been as strong as ever. Even so, she couldn't blame him for walking away afterwards when she had been well aware of his womanising reputation.

But she *did* very much blame Angel for his attitude when she had confronted him with her pregnancy. She didn't care that he had been taken by surprise. She had no sympathy for him on that score and much more sympathy for herself, walking round the size of a barrel for months on end while agonising about how she was to cope and survive as a single parent. And then the father of her baby had flatly refused to accept *his* share of the responsibility and had shot her down in mortifying flames. It would be a cold day in hell before she forgave Angel for that crushing rejection!

'Gaby?' Clara murmured from behind her. 'I've put Alexios up for his nap and I'm heading out to the greenhouse.'

Gaby whirled round, taken aback to see Clara now clad in her outdoor jacket and boots. 'OK…'

Angel appeared behind the older woman and Gaby's jaw simply dropped at the sight of him indoors rather than outside where he should still have been.

'I brought your visitor in through the back,' her employer and friend informed her quietly. 'You need to talk…and not through a closed door.'

Angel surveyed her with hidden fascination, unable to forget how long it had taken and how hard it had been to find her again. He could feel untamed emotion buzzing through him and that annoyed him when he needed to be in cool control of himself, unlike his parents, who had never been in control or even accepted that they ought to be.

Flags of embarrassed colour had flown into Gabriella's already flushed face, Angel noted appreciatively. He didn't think there could be a woman alive who could look as beautiful as she did without making the smallest effort to do so. There she stood, blue eyes burning bright, utterly enraged by him, in a shabby old pastel-pink sweater and faded jeans, both of which clung to her mesmerising curves like a second skin. For a split second, Angel forgot why he was there, forgot their audience, forgot everything and almost reached for her like a hot, thirsty man tempted by a drink of water. In terms of sexual need, he reasoned grimly, he was both hotly aroused and *very* thirsty. Annoyance at his masculine predictability chilled his overheated blood and he tilted his arrogant dark head back to study Gabriella with an assessing look. Was she the mother of his son...*or not*?

'Well, I won't say that that wasn't embarrassing,' Gaby breathed tightly as she marched past him back into the living area.

'Since the lady appears to know who I am, will she be discreet?' Angel enquired.

And that fast, Gaby wanted to thump him again. 'Of course she will be. Clara isn't remotely interested in you or in publicity,' she pronounced curtly. 'What are you doing here? What do you want from me?'

'I would like to see the child,' Angel intoned without any expression at all. Gaby interpreted that as Angel, *unusually*, watching his every word.

'You said that child was nothing to do with you!' Gaby reminded him.

'May we sit down and discuss this important matter?'

'You're asking me to be reasonable when you were not remotely reasonable with me nine months ago?' Gaby launched at him incredulously. 'I can't believe your nerve!'

The smooth, hard planes of his lean bronzed features were impassive, infuriatingly uninformative. 'You've said that to me before.'

'Yes…' Gaby compressed her lips on the reminder.

'It could be…' Angel breathed in deep and slow '…that I was a little hasty at our last meeting.'

A spasm of intense satisfaction arrowed

through Gaby at that unexpected admission from Angel. 'A little hasty? Is that so?'

Picking up on her pleasure at his discomfiture, Angel gritted his even white teeth. 'Yes, that is so. As you pointed out at the time, there is always risk attached to sexual intimacy.'

'I do not view the conception of my son as a risk.'

Angel shrugged a cashmere-clad broad shoulder, seemingly indifferent to her sensitivity, his hard, handsome face unyielding. 'I should have acknowledged at the time that there was a chance that I could be responsible, but I had already been through this scenario with one too many of your predecessors with the result that I was too angry to be logical. My background has made it a challenge for me to trust women.'

Gaby did not like being included in the category of 'predecessors' but her curiosity was piqued by his admission that he found it difficult to trust her sex. 'It was one night,' she conceded with a careless shrug that in no way mirrored how she felt about it. 'Now that you're apologising, I suppose I can follow your feelings to some degree.'

'I was not aware that I was apologising,' Angel framed grittily.

'If you're not prepared to apologise for the

way you treated me that day at the hotel, I have nothing more to say to you,' she told him truthfully. 'Nobody treats me like that and gets away with it!'

Angel ground his teeth together again.

'You see, I understand that you're rude because you're used to people tiptoeing around your royal person, but your birth and your wealth do not mean that you are better than I am,' Gaby spelt out succinctly. 'Or that I will let you get away with behaving as though you are.'

Angel's brilliant dark golden eyes smouldered as though she had lit a fire behind them. 'Message received,' Angel murmured dulcetly, disconcerting her with that easy switch. 'I apologise for treating you unfairly.'

Gaby hadn't believed that he would or even could climb down off his high horse and the shock of that accomplishment knocked her off balance. 'All right…so let's move on. Why do you want to see Alexios? Surely you would want DNA testing before doing so?'

'Is it true that he has green eyes?' Angel demanded, startling her with that apparently random question.

'Yes, it is…but what does that have to do with anything? And how did you track me down here anyway?' Gaby pressed in a ruffled tone.

'Let me give you a hint…you've been too active on social media with your friends. I've been searching for you for months,' Angel revealed. 'There were no leads until I was able to establish a link between Laurie Bannister, your friend Liz's twin, and you. From that point it was possible to check out their connections to find out where you might be.'

'What do you mean by searching?' Gaby prompted in dismay at what he had revealed. It was true that she had often chatted to Liz's twin, Laurie, online, mentioning meetings because Laurie lived only forty miles away with her husband.

'If your son is also *my* son, we have a situation which I cannot ignore. He would not be an ordinary child—he would be a *royal* child. It was imperative that I locate you and check it out. I used a private detective agency to trace you.'

'Through my friends,' she repeated in horror. 'You had someone snoop into *their* lives to track *me* down? That's appalling.'

'If you had left a forwarding address or told your friend Liz that it was acceptable to tell me where you were, we wouldn't be in this position now and I wouldn't have had to have anyone investigated,' Angel countered without hesitation.

Gaby studied a scratched area of the pine kitchen table, mastering her resentment. It was done and too late to complain about anyone's privacy being invaded, she conceded grudgingly. Perhaps telling Liz not to share her address, should Angel enquire, had been a step too far in mistrust…and he had enquired through staff. But then, she recognised ruefully, she had wanted to *punish* him, an urge which Clara's intervention had reminded her that she needed to suppress.

'Look,' she said stiffly. 'Come into the… er…sitting room…' Walking back across the hall, she pushed open the door of the room that was hardly ever used, crossing to the window to lift the blind and let in the sunlight. 'Do you still drink black coffee with one sugar?'

Angel released his pent-up breath, registering that Gabriella wasn't going to shout or throw things at him again. The strangest sense of disappointment instantly afflicted him and took him aback. No woman had ever argued with him or criticised him the way that Gabriella did and why the hell would he miss that?

'Yes, thank you,' he murmured with scrupulous politeness.

Angel sounded smooth as glass and Gaby shot him a suspicious glance, wondering what manipulative thoughts were currently operating behind that wickedly attractive façade of his. As she had learned in the past, he was clever, *very* clever, and well able to play the long game to conceal his true purpose. But just then she had more on her mind than working out Angel's motivation and she bent to light the gas fire in the chilly room before speeding off to check on Clara and make the coffee.

She could have taken Angel up to the small apartment above the extension where she lived but that would take him too close to her son and she wasn't ready for that step yet. So, instead of that she put on the kettle and hurried out to the greenhouse to see Clara.

'We're in the sitting room, so you don't need to stay out here if you don't want to,' she told the older woman gently. 'Sorry about the shouting. I'm afraid Angel tends to send my temper sky-high.'

'I reckon his temper is every bit as bad as yours but he's too reserved to let it fly,' Clara surmised as she worked at her bench, potting up seedlings. 'He's much too handsome for his own good, and he'll be a truckload of trouble, but I suspect he might be worth it. Only you can decide if he is.'

'He's only here because he is finally accepting that Alexios could be his,' Gaby muttered unhappily.

'Whatever happens, you mustn't get into a hostile relationship with him.'

'How could it be anything other than hostile?' Gaby's lovely face was strained as she hovered in the greenhouse doorway.

'It *has* to be something else for your son's sake. Boys need a father,' Clara informed her.

Paling, Gaby walked back indoors to make the coffee. Be polite, be civilised, she instructed herself, stop making it all so personal and emotional. Wasn't that a dead giveaway of how Angel made her feel? Getting all riled up and shouting? She was making it far too obvious that she was emotionally involved and had been wounded by the fallout of that night in Alharia. Gaby flinched at the thought and reminded herself that she had been a consenting adult, who had believed that she knew exactly what she was doing. It was a little late now to acknowledge that she had fooled herself into reaching for what she thought she wanted only to discover afterwards that she had secretly wanted much more than a brief sexual encounter...

Angel was cold and he stood by the fire, which put out a miserable amount of heat. He checked his watch, regretting that he had to be back on Themos by morning to attend an important event. He needed time to deal with Gabriella and he didn't have time to spare. In any case, he was naturally impatient, he conceded, a muscle tightening at his strong jaw as he struggled to clamp down on the volatile mix of anger, frustration and desire that Gabriella always evoked.

Her reappearance with a tray almost made him laugh. Gabriella serving him graciously with coffee was not a vision that rose easily to his imagination. He grasped the cup.

'Months ago, you joked on social media about having a child with green eyes and curly hair,' Angel remarked tautly.

Gaby lifted a brow. 'And the significance of that…is?'

'My mother had green eyes and curls. She was a legendary beauty. Queen Nabila. Look her up online,' Angel urged forbiddingly, as though the subject were distasteful to him.

And, of course, on his terms it *had* to be distasteful to contemplate the likelihood of his first child having been accidentally born to an ordinary woman not of his choosing. Both his parents had been born into royal families and he knew nothing else.

'But that could just be coincidence,' Gaby heard herself declare because, when push came to shove, she was realising that she was not eager to share her little boy with Angel. No doubt that was selfish but that was how she felt. Alexios was her family now and, having lost her family when she was fourteen, she was particularly keen now to hold her son close.

'Do you have reason to believe that your son could have been fathered by someone else?' Angel queried curtly. 'Were you with any other man shortly before or soon after me?'

A tide of angry red flooded up her throat into her cheeks. 'There was no other man. You were my first...' and her voice ran out of angry steam on that admission because she had not meant to tell him that much.

Angel's ebony brows pleated in consternation. 'Your...*first*? Are you serious?'

'Wish I wasn't but *yes*,' Gaby confirmed with bitter force.

'I wouldn't have taken you to bed had I known that,' Angel breathed in a driven undertone, swinging away from her to stand by the window and stare out, his strong profile taut and set. 'I don't mess around with virgins. It's too inequal, too open to misinterpretation.'

'Not in my case,' Gaby said dulcetly. 'I knew what I was getting and I got it.'

Angel flipped back to her, sizzling dark golden eyes bright as the sun. 'And what's that supposed to mean?' he flared back at her, sensing that he was being insulted.

'A guy who wouldn't even wake me up to say goodbye.'

Angel visibly ground his even white teeth together and then froze to say, '*No*, we're not doing this! You're not going to derail me from the reason I'm here by making me angry again,' he told her harshly. 'And I'm here to ask if you will agree to a private DNA test being done.'

Gaby recalled how he had thrown it in her face that *she* would drag *him* to court to demand a DNA test. 'No.'

Angel's gaze narrowed, hardened. 'Then we go through the courts.'

Gaby paled at that immediate rejoinder. 'No, there's no good reason to take it that far.'

'Yes, there is. If your child is mine, then I will have to marry you!' Angel bit out rawly.

Gaby's dark blue eyes widened to their fullest extent and she stared back at him in disbelief. 'Now it's my turn to a-ask if you are serious,' she stammered unevenly.

'Serious as a heart attack,' Angel qualified without a shade of amusement.

CHAPTER FIVE

THE MUG OF coffee in Gaby's hand trembled and she sank down into an armchair. 'You'd have to *marry* me?'

Angel swallowed hard. He would have to marry her to ensure his child was properly protected from damaging influences. After his own childhood experiences, he would *have* to be directly involved in the raising of his own child because the alternative would be, to his mind, a sin. He accepted that bringing up his child was his duty, but he also knew that, thanks to his own dysfunctional background, he had not a clue how to be a good husband or father, which was rather daunting. He studied Gabriella, striving to read her reaction to what he had said, but her jewel-blue eyes were unrevealing and she looked more shocked than anything else.

'We're jumping the gun,' he acknowledged.

'First, will you agree to the DNA test and will you allow me to see him?'

Gaby swallowed so hard she hurt her throat. 'Explain why you said that you would *have* to marry me,' she prompted tightly.

'My firstborn son is the heir to the throne.'

'But we're not married!' she protested.

'We don't have to be according to the constitution of Themos in which the firstborn son inherits. In the seventeenth century one of my ancestors was unable to have children with his wife but he already had a son by his mistress and his son took the throne after him. His father changed the rules to keep the Diamandis family in power. Married or not, if your son is mine, he will be my heir,' Angel explained flatly. 'And if I marry you, you will eventually be the Queen of Themos, ruling by my side.'

'For goodness' sake…' Gaby set down her coffee and released a deep sigh. 'I had no idea. I didn't even think Alexios could ever be the heir to anything that belonged to you,' she framed truthfully.

'If you're telling me the truth and I was your only lover, he won't be illegitimate for very long because our marriage would legitimise his birth,' Angel breathed tautly. 'So, the DNA test?'

'I suppose I don't have much choice on that

score because it wouldn't be fair to you or my son to refuse. On that basis I'll go along with it,' Gaby muttered uneasily.

'I'll make the arrangements,' Angel told her as he pulled out his phone, speaking in fast idiomatic Italian to whoever was at the other end of the line, an employee, she decided, because Angel was reeling off instructions. Someone was to come to the house to perform the DNA test and fast-track the results back to him.

He dug his phone back into the pocket of his cashmere coat and raked long brown fingers through the luxuriant ebony hair brushing his brow, tousling it. Her breath snarled up in her throat as he glanced back at her through a fringe of inky spiky lashes, his eyes a simmering slash of gold as hot as the heart of a fire, his lean, strong jaw framed and enhanced by black stubble. Her body came to life as though he had flipped a switch, her breasts tightening inside her bra, a tugging sensation clenching the heart of her. She shifted uncomfortably in her seat, her colour heightening.

I will have to marry you? Not words she had ever expected Angel to say to her personally, not even in some crazy fantasy. Even as a teenaged student she had never dreamt big enough to imagine herself marrying a royal prince. But why would he *have* to marry her? Because Alexios was his heir? Surely if legitimacy were not demanded, marriage would be unnecessary? She could not, even in the wildest reaches of her imagination, picture being married to Angel, whose lifestyle was so far removed from her own. Themos was a very glamorous place, packed with the rich, famous and powerful. The island teemed with yachts, luxury hotels and casinos and staged world-class fashion, sport and charity events. Nobody would match someone as ordinary as she was to someone like Angel, the ruler of his own little country.

'May I see him?' Angel pressed.

Gaby's lips parted to utter a negative but then she thought about it. She already knew that Alexios was Angel's flesh and blood and soon *he* would know as well. What good reason did she now have to refuse him access to a mere glimpse of his sleeping son?

'OK, but you'll have to be very quiet. He's cross as tacks if you wake him in the middle of a nap,' Gaby warned, leaving him to follow her back across the hall into the kitchen, where a small corner staircase led up to her little apartment.

'What are you doing living here?' Angel asked.

'Clara had knee surgery and needed someone around to help until she was mobile again. Alexios was a newborn. This arrangement suits us both because we both still have our privacy. In a few weeks, Clara will be moving into a smaller house in town, which will suit her better, and Alexios and I will be moving on.'

'To where?'

'I haven't decided because Clara doesn't have an actual moving date yet.' Gaby opened the door of her accommodation at the top of the stairs. 'Her son lived here until he emigrated.'

Angel thought the large room with its shabby furniture and small kitchen area at the far end was a dump. He paused by the one connecting door. 'Is the child in here?' he prompted.

Her face taut, Gaby stepped past him to open the door quietly and step into her bedroom, which she shared with her son. As luck would have it, Alexios was already awake, sitting up in one corner of his crib, hugging his rabbit blankie. A huge welcoming grin lit up his little face when he saw her. Behind her, she heard Angel release his breath in a sudden hiss.

'He has my mother's eyes,' Angel whispered hoarsely. 'And he looks very like baby pictures of me.'

'Surprise, surprise,' Gaby said drily as she bent down to lift the child already holding his arms up in anticipation. 'I did tell you he was yours.'

Angel tensed as she spun back round to face him. He wasn't comfortable with young children. None of his friends had had kids yet. Nobody handed him a baby and expected him to know what to do with it...but Gaby *did*. She plonked the child into Angel's arms as though he were a parental veteran.

Angel stared into those vivid green eyes that reminded him so disturbingly of his late mother. His son smiled and planted a chubby little hand against the stubble surrounding Angel's mouth, fingers exploring that interesting roughness. The baby giggled.

'He's not used to men, so you'll be a novelty,' Gaby remarked, feeling that in the circumstances she was being remarkably generous in sharing her son.

That innocent chuckle released Angel's tension. A smile flashed across his wide sensual mouth and Gaby's heart stuttered in receipt of that powerful flare of raw masculine charisma. Illuminated by that smile, his lean, darkly handsome features were incredibly appealing.

'He seems to be a happy baby.'

'He is. Why wouldn't he be? There are no problems in his little world.' Gaby moved back out of the bedroom. 'Do you want to play with him?'

Angel winced. 'I wouldn't know how to. You called him Alexios?'

'It's Greek.' Gaby coloured with self-consciousness.

'My great-grandfather was also called Alexios,' Angel remarked.

'Was he?' Gaby lifted and dropped a shoulder, refusing to be drawn as she reclaimed her son. She settled down on the rug with him and pulled over a plastic basket of toys. 'Come on,' she murmured ruefully. 'You have to learn how to play with him some time.'

Angel, the picture of elegance in his designer silk-and-wool-blend charcoal-grey suit worn beneath his coat, froze and gave her a startled glance. 'Right now?'

Gaby settled sapphire-blue eyes that gleamed on him. 'Now would be a good time. It's the easiest way to make him relax with you.'

Angel shed his coat and dropped down into the nearest armchair with the air of a condemned man.

Gaby disregarded his absence of enthusiasm. Angel did not like to be ignorant in any field. Anything that made him vulnerable seemed to put him on edge, but she wanted to see if he could make an effort and unbend for Alexios's benefit. She piled up bricks and Alexios sent them flying with exuberance. She settled a toy lorry into his lap, which he lifted to chew.

'Shouldn't you take that off him?' Angel enquired.

'No. Everything goes in his mouth at present. He's teething,' Gaby told him, trying not to stare as Angel inched forward off the chair much as though he were approaching a snapping shark and settled a plastic car on the rug in front of her son.

Angel made what she deemed to be 'boy' noises with the car and Alexios was delighted. From that point on she might as well have not been there for all the attention she received from her two companions and Gaby quietly left them to it, busying herself by making her son's lunch.

'He's falling asleep,' Angel complained.

'He will…he didn't have his usual nap,' Gaby reminded him, amused by his tone of disappointment. Alexios was a novelty for

Angel and it worked both ways, Gaby conceded wryly. Men often played in a different way with babies than women did and Alexios had enjoyed Angel's more physical, noisy approach. She wasn't jealous of the bond she had seen developing between father and son because she could see how beneficial it would be for her child. 'But try to keep him awake. I still have to feed him.'

'And then perhaps we could talk…'

'There's not a lot to talk about… I mean, that reference to marriage was just pure insanity,' Gaby told him irritably as she busied herself in the little kitchen area. 'We'd probably kill each other by the end of the first month!'

'But what a way to go…' Angel husked, disconcerting her with that purred sensual response.

Sidestepping that inappropriate comment, Gaby picked up Alexios and slotted him into his high chair, attaching a bib and lifting the feeding dish. 'Let's stick to basics here. If you want a relationship with Alexios, I'm not planning to stand in the way.'

'It was premature to refer to marriage. I shouldn't have opened with the subject,' Angel cut in smoothly.

And that interruption convinced Gaby that he had never meant to mention marriage in the first place, which made much better sense to her. In the heat of the moment, he had got carried away. Her tense shoulders relaxed a little as she fed Alexios, making aeroplane noises and gestures with the spoon to keep him awake.

'I don't have any lunch to offer you,' she told Angel awkwardly. 'Clara and I usually have a snack rather than a meal.'

'Not a problem. I have to leave soon. I have an event to attend at home first thing tomorrow morning.'

Instead of feeling relieved by the reference to his departure, Gaby felt a sense of loss and hated herself. All right, Angel had been a colourful addition to her day, but she shouldn't have any personal reaction to him. The drama was over, a DNA test would be done, presumably fences would be mended for the sake of peace and Angel would become an occasional visitor in his son's life, she reasoned, censuring herself for getting more than superficially involved in his arrival.

Angel watched her tuck her sleepy son back into his cot. His proximity unnerved her. The room seemed to shrink around her as she brushed past him and closed the door. The faint tang of his cologne assailed her, firing memories of that night in Alharia, and she jerked back another step, accidentally knocking her hip against the wall.

'You're so jumpy around me,' Angel remarked.

Unwarily, Gaby glanced up and was immediately ensnared by dark golden eyes that burned through her defences like hot lava. 'Do you blame me? I mean, after what happened between us in Alharia?' she extended uncomfortably.

'No regrets this side of the fence, *glykia mou*,' Angel husked, staring down at her, the luxuriant black tangle of his lashes intensifying his stunning gaze. 'I'm no hypocrite. It was an extraordinary night.'

'Oh, *please*, like I believe that after the number of such encounters that you must have had!' Gaby riposted helplessly, breathless and taut in spite of every effort to remain unaffected by him.

'Extraordinary and unforgettable,' Angel repeated in defiance of that charge as he backed her into the wall, suddenly dangerously close and as dangerously intent on her as a tiger that had been provoked.

A ripple of awareness that was so highly charged that it almost *hurt* travelled through her slender frame. Her breasts felt constrained by her bra, the sensitive tips pushing to prominence against the scratchy lace while a clenching sensation tugged in her pelvis. Hot colour flooded her cheeks at that wholly primitive response that had nothing to do with logic and she trembled.

Angel scored a gentle fingertip across her cheekbone, his gaze molten gold with hunger, and it was too much for her in the mood she was in, all the emotional distress his appearance had evoked fusing with a desire she could not suppress. Stretching up on tiptoe, she claimed his wide sensual mouth for herself. He tasted of mint and fresh air and sunshine and a raw need that reverberated through her like a lightning strike. His mouth crushed hers and she felt as though she was collapsing into him until he edged her back against the wall for support. His tongue delved and liquid fire stabbed through her and that fast she wanted to rip his clothes off…

Her fingers dug into his shoulders, laced into his thick black hair. The fine fabric of his trousers couldn't conceal the bold thrust of his erection against her midriff and her hand travelled down over his chest to trace the throbbing evidence of his arousal. He groaned under his breath, pushing against her, tugging at the waistband of her jeans, pushing down the zip.

Their mutual hunger was frantic, uncontrolled. There was nothing seemly about it, she would later concede when she thought back to that moment and shuddered with embarrassment. But right then the allure of the forbidden sucked her right in and swallowed her alive. The brush of his fingers against her stomach was familiar, the less innocent slide of his hand beneath her knickers desperately desired and his carnal touch there, where she ached most of all, unbearably exciting. She pushed against him and quivered, helplessly enthralled by the demands of her own body, her heart racing and her blood thrumming with a wild insistent beat in her veins. Desire had caught her in a steely, unbreakable hold and with every plunge of his wicked tongue and every stroke of his hand her defences splintered and weakened. Her sensation-starved body surged to a feverish peak at his command alone. In climax, she jerked and gasped and then gasped again, pleasure claiming her in long, tingling waves.

'You drive me…*insane*,' Angel groaned just as her jeans began to slide down her thighs.

In that same instant a mobile phone buzzed loudly and he looked at her and she looked at him and just when she believed that he would ignore his phone, he glanced down at his watch instead and suddenly swore in ragged Greek. 'If I don't leave now, the jet will miss our flight slot!' he bit out in raw frustration.

Gaby turned crimson and yanked up her jeans, her feminine core still pulsing and her nipples as hard as bullets. She had craved sex with Angel as much as though he were an addictive drug. She couldn't believe what she had almost done, and her sole consolation was that a glance at Angel's unconcealed tension and discomfiture confirmed that he too was full of incomprehension at what had almost transpired. Up against the wall as well, she reflected sickly, like a wanton desperate hussy.

'Throw me out before I do something worse,' he urged in a driven undertone, brilliant eyes shielded by his lashes to glittering stars in darkness. 'You destroy my self-discipline…'

And she had no discipline whatsoever around him either, Gaby acknowledged with sudden shamed bitterness as she led the way back downstairs to the separate front door she rarely utilised to speed his departure. This time, however, he took her phone number.

'The test will be done within forty-eight hours,' he promised her before he stepped back over the wall and climbed back into the helicopter. 'I'll be in touch.'

And that was that, but she was shell-shocked, deeply shaken by that encounter. Angel had played with Alexios and had warmed up to their son in a way she had not known he was capable of achieving. Angel was so shuttered, so locked up in himself most of the time, and that arrogant, bold surface gloss of his usually hid the fact from the world. It was a challenge for him to loosen up, to relax his guard and yet he had done it for a baby's benefit. He had done silly things to amuse Alexios and that had touched Gaby in the most unexpected way. Would that willingness to get down to a child's level last? Would her son truly become Angel's heir? For good? Or just until Angel married and had another male child with a carefully chosen royal wife?

Those were questions and concerns that were still troubling Gaby while she walked up the gentle hill behind the farm on an afternoon six days later. She was taking a break because Alexios was having his nap and Clara had friends in for lunch.

Within twenty-four hours of Angel's visit, a technician had arrived to perform the DNA test and in due course Angel had texted Gaby to confirm that Alexios was *his* son…as if she had ever been in any doubt of that fact! She had to wonder why he had bothered to send that text without sending an unreserved apology with it because the year before, when she had approached him with her pregnancy, he had treated her like a gold-digging, publicity-seeking fraudster. Did he regret that now? Did he wish he had listened, *believed* her? Or did the ruling Prince of Themos not concern himself with such trivia as his past mistakes?

As she reached the top of the hill and stood looking out at the view, a helicopter swooped down to land in the field fronting the farmhouse. A tall man sprang out and her nervous tension rocketed as high as the skyline as she began to move back towards the house. Within minutes, the same figure reappeared and passed through the gate behind the farm to start moving in her direction. Her breath shortened in her throat and her pace slowed as she recognised that the visitor striding through the rough field grass towards her was indeed Angel. Why on earth was he here again so soon after his last visit?

'Gabriella…' Angel hailed her long before he reached her, black hair tousled by the breeze above his lean bronzed face, dark eyes narrowed to focus on her with noticeable intensity. Shockingly spectacular, shockingly sexy. He stopped several feet away, an incongruous picture in his designer suit against the backdrop of a windblown field.

'I was coming back to the house,' Gaby muttered uncomfortably, feeling rumpled and messy in the face of his habitually immaculate presentation.

'We can walk back together.'

Gaby shot him a fleeting look of frustration. 'What are you doing here again?'

With sheer force of will, Angel held that darting evasive glance of hers, dark golden eyes flaring bright. 'You should know why I'm here. I did warn you. Alexios is my son, and we will have to get married. The sooner we do the deed, the sooner life can settle down again and the less chance there will be for the press to make a spectacle of us and our child,' he concluded grimly.

'But you *can't* be serious about us getting married?' Gaby argued, her steps faltering as she turned round to face him.

'I'm deadly serious,' Angel contradicted.

'But why?'

'Your son's future is in Themos and I will not allow you to deprive him of his birthright and heritage,' Angel countered without hesitation.

An angry flush mantling her cheeks, Gaby flung her head back, copper strands sliding back from her face to accentuate her fine bone structure. 'I have no intention of depriving my son of anything that he *needs*!' she stressed.

'That's good, because he needs his father just as much as he needs his mother,' Angel slotted in glibly.

'What a shame you didn't feel that way last year when I approached you!' Gaby framed furiously. 'If you had *listened* to me then, you would have had much more time to decide how *we* should move forward as parents, and I very much doubt that you would have come up with anything as crazy as marriage being the solution!'

'Leave the past where it belongs and concentrate on our child for the moment,' Angel urged with a rapier-sharp edge to his intonation. 'Right now, Alexios is our most important concern. Let me tell you, I am determined that my son will have a far better and happier start to life than I ever had!'

'That's all very well,' Gaby muttered, taken aback by that sudden shadowy revelation about his own childhood and tucking it away for later examination. 'But marriage between us is *not* the solution.'

'I will be straight. It is either marriage or a custody case because I will fight you through the courts before I risk allowing my son to grow up without daily access to the country which is his!' Angel sliced back at her, stealing the breath from her lungs and freezing her in place while he strode back towards the farmhouse.

In fear, Gaby shook off her nervous paralysis and chased after him. 'You don't mean that, you *can't*!' she protested. 'Would you really try to take Alexios away from me? Are you really that cruel?'

'I would do it with great regret because a loving mother is a huge gift and I have no desire to separate you from each other. On the other hand, Alexios belongs with his father as well and if we cannot agree a compromise, I would have no choice but to fight you.'

'And…the only available compromise is *marriage*?' Gaby almost whispered, pale as death now.

'Yes. That way he has both of us and we share him, and he grows up in the country which he will one day rule,' Angel conceded, the harsher edge to his deep dark drawl easing a little. 'He will be my priority in life… I promise you that. I will be a parent in every way possible to him. There is *nothing* that he will lack…'

Wholly taken aback now by that passionate declaration of his parental intentions from a man whom she had once naively assumed couldn't care less about such matters, Gaby swallowed hard and said nothing, which of course turned out to be a mistake when Angel continued speaking.

'Perhaps it would be easier for you to give him up altogether and get on with your life, unrestricted by our son's status,' he intoned, shocking her even more with that suggestion. 'A royal life is full of restrictions and I believe you have less interest in such a lifestyle than many women I've known.'

Gaby blinked while she tried to think fast about the horrible options he was putting before her. 'All these years and that's the very first compliment you have ever given me that didn't relate to my looks.'

Angel frowned. 'No, I'm not that superficial.'

'With me, you were, but maybe you're always like that with women,' Gaby remarked with a dismissive shrug. 'I'm afraid I'm not prepared to walk away from Alexios even though I suspect that that option might suit you the best.'

'Even though his mother walking away would *break* my son's heart?' Angel breathed with incredulous bite. 'You don't think much of me, do you? I would never wish such hurt on my son as abandonment by a parent would bring. It happened in my own family and the pain of it resonates even in adulthood.'

Gaby felt as though she had been thoroughly scolded. Her pallor was chased off by a guilty flush while she wondered who had been abandoned in childhood in his family circle. 'Who in your family did that happen to?'

Angel's lean dark features tensed. 'That is a private family matter I cannot discuss with you.'

Gaby reddened and looked away again. 'Let me sum up what you've said. According to you my choices are pretty basic. Marriage or a court battle? Not much room to negotiate there.'

'Yes,' Angel confirmed. 'But there is no viable alternative.'

Gaby chewed her lip to ensure that she didn't erupt into a flood of exasperated disagreement. In a world where single parents were commonplace, of course there were alternatives, only he was not prepared to consider them. And she didn't feel that she was in a strong enough or safe enough position to risk angering Angel by fighting bitterly with him. Angel would make a terrifying enemy, and not only because of his stubborn, arrogant and implacable character, but also because of his standing in the world. He was incredibly rich, and he enjoyed diplomatic status. He also had many friends in high places. In a court case centred on a child with a royal birthright, a child who was undeniably important to the country he would one day rule, how could she be sure how such a judgement would go? Mothers did not automatically retain custody of their children in all circumstances. Mothers could and indeed did lose their children if the father were deemed to be the more suitable parent to have custody. Angel might well fit that category when, one day, Alexios would become King.

'If it's a choice between a custody battle and marriage, I'll go for marriage,' Gaby murmured tightly, resisting the urge to point out that, in her opinion, he was not actually giving her a choice that she could reasonably be expected to think about.

Angel flashed her a sudden brilliant smile, relief lightening his unusually expressive dark golden eyes. 'It's the right decision,' he assured her.

'But that still leaves us a lot of stuff to talk about,' Gaby pointed out.

'No, it doesn't,' Angel stated with his usual

confidence. 'Once we're married, everything will fall naturally into place.'

'Yes, what about…the other hundred and one things that matter in a marriage?' Gaby pressed urgently.

'We will be a normal couple…*and* we will be a family like other normal families.' Angel had difficulty putting into words exactly what he wanted for his son, but the word 'normal' kept on cropping up along with his highest hopes, reminding him that nothing about his own childhood had been remotely normal… at least, only normal for a severely dysfunctional family.

Angel knew that he was struggling to find words because on many levels he was in turmoil. He had only just discovered that he was a father and to some degree that was terrifying when he looked back at how much his own parents had let *him* down as a child. He knew that he would have to make a lot of sacrifices to be a decent parent. He would have to be there for the big things like birthdays and the little things like learning to swim. He would have to be there when life was good, but he would have to be there even more for his child when his life was difficult. Too often, proud independence had forced Angel as a child to hide his problems and struggle to deal with them alone.

Guilt pierced him when he remembered how he had rejected Gabriella when she was pregnant, when his care for his child and his child's mother *should* have begun. He had already failed them once, he could not, would not, do it ever again. He wanted Gabriella, but control with a woman was everything, he reasoned. As long as that sexual desire didn't get out of hand or threaten to turn into anything that would put him at risk of foolishness, it would be fine, he assured himself.

Gaby studied him in shock at that announcement he had made. 'But there's nothing normal about the life you lead.'

'That life of self-indulgence is over,' Angel told her almost harshly. 'Alexios will come first in all things. I want him to be happy in a family setting.'

'Yes, of course, but what about all the women you currently run about with?' Gaby vented between clenched teeth as they reached the farmhouse.

'For once in your life, could you practise optimism?' Angel cut in reprovingly. 'Could you expect the best from me instead of only the worst? I can do faithful if I have to.'

Gaby was in absolute shock at the awareness that she had agreed to become Angel's wife, even while she knew that she would sooner not have been the catalyst for Angel saying that he could do faithful if he *had* to. There was nothing normal about that constraint and she wondered how to tell him that creating a normal family would not be easy for a man from his very different background unless he was willing to make enormous sacrifices. Why? Angel had never in his life had to respect limits. As far as she knew he had always done exactly as he liked, and he had done so from a terrifyingly early age. How on earth did he imagine that he would give up the freedom and variety of his very active sex life with uber-glamorous women?

And how on earth could someone who, by the sounds of it, had never known normal in his own childhood declare that he would provide it for Alexios? It was annoying not to know more about his background and troubling that he was so secretive on that topic. The inner conflict he was so determined to conceal only increased her curiosity while his willingness to change his life to best accommodate their son's needs could only impress her.

CHAPTER SIX

'*THIS* IS THE LIFE!' Liz declared with a wicked grin as she nestled back in an opulent leather seat on the Diamandis private jet and saluted her sister, Laurie, and Gaby with a cocktail glass in her hand. 'I give you a toast—to the woman that broke the mould and exceeded all possible expectations, who is about to become a *royal* princess!'

'Pretty sure you just set feminism back by a century or two!' Laurie groaned for her twin. 'No, but I will toast Gaby for her power in getting a commitment-phobic prince to the altar! I think that's the real achievement here.'

'Alexios…' Gaby reminded her friend gently.

'Your prince isn't so slow that he couldn't have wriggled out of marriage if he had wanted to,' Liz opined. 'You set far too low a value on your own worth.'

'Gaby, *nobody* was immune to Angel's attraction at university and loads of women chased him. You're the only one *he* had to chase that I know of and the only one who ditched him!' Laurie told her with unhidden pride.

Gaby smiled with as much affectionate amusement as she could muster, full of regret that she could no longer be as frank as she had once been with her friends. She bent down to secure Alexios into his seat because the jet was about to land on Themos. It was not that she didn't trust her friends not to betray her, more that she felt that her son's privacy had to be protected and family secrets fell under that same label. The true background to the royal wedding due to take place in forty-eight hours would go to the grave with her, she decided morbidly. She hoped she would never be bitter enough to expose Alexios to the reality of his father's ruthlessness. When it had come down to marriage or running the risk that she might, at the very least, lose full-time custody of her son, Gaby had crumbled, and the matrimonial option had won. Angel had subjected her to his version of a shotgun marriage…

Unfortunately, exposure to Angel generally made her feel that she was weaker than she should be. He was blackmailing her, but she was still fiercely attracted to him and fascinated by him. She suspected that she would always want more than Angel would give her: feelings as opposed to orgasms. Although the latter were wonderful, she craved a stronger connection with him.

Only three weeks had flown by since that final epic meeting with him in Scotland. Everything that had happened during those weeks had exceeded Gaby's wildest expectations. Angel had phoned her every day, but generally only to ask random questions about Alexios or advance information she needed to know about the wedding arrangements.

A lawyer had arrived with a pre-nuptial contract for her to peruse and had advised her to obtain her own independent advice. Gaby had instead read it cover to cover. Aside from Angel's conviction that he should keep her in the lap of luxury for the rest of her days regardless of how she behaved, and his desire for Alexios and therefore Gaby, as his mother, to remain on Themos, even in the wake of divorce, she had found nothing untoward in the conditions. It had proved to be a practical, businesslike document and she had signed without further ado.

A woman from a famous fashion studio had flown from Paris to Clara's house to measure Gaby up for a wedding gown and to give her a preview of exclusive models and accessories.

As her matrons of honour, Laurie and Liz had also been included in that procedure at their own homes. The extravagance of such an approach to staging a wedding within so short a time space had stunned all of them.

Clara had received an invitation but had opted not to attend, insisting that she would enjoy her goddaughters' photos and descriptions of the event more. With her husband currently working abroad, Laurie would be replacing Gaby and helping Clara move into her new home. Gaby's fiercely ambitious aunt, Janine, who was working towards a partnership in her legal firm, had decided that she couldn't afford to take time off to see her niece married, and Gaby had not been surprised by that unsentimental decision. Janine's driving force had always been her career.

'Oh, my word, look at those beaches!' Laurie proclaimed and Gaby peered out of the nearest window to see a disorientating blur of tree-lined coves with shimmering golden sands meeting a turquoise sea before the jet swung over land again and she glimpsed buildings and trees. Anticipation blossomed inside her.

The unbelievable opulence of Angel's private jet, where the three women had been waited on hand and foot from the instant they boarded, had startled Gaby, who wasn't accustomed to frills or even treats. She had gone from being a teenager always short of cash, and trying to conceal the fact, to an adult who saved constantly for a rainy day...and her rainy day had been pregnancy and motherhood, which had emptied her savings account.

The jet landed at Leveus, the capital city of Themos. An official came on board to check their documentation and then ushered them out into a limousine waiting right beside the jet to pick them up. The hot sun enveloped her, golden and warm on her skin, and Gaby soaked it up.

'Yes, definitely the dream life,' Liz proclaimed with a grin. 'Glorious sunshine. No queues, no baggage worries, no waiting for transport. All the hassle has been smoothed away for your benefit.'

'And there's no chance of paparazzi stealing a first view of the bride-to-be and the heir,' Laurie completed with satisfaction.

'The paps aren't allowed to operate on Themos,' Gaby explained, turning pink when her companions looked at her in surprise that she should know such a fact. 'They've been banned on the island because there are so many famous residents here, keen to protect their privacy.'

'Someone's been doing their homework,' Laurie teased.

'Of course I have,' Gaby confirmed as the limo filtered into a traffic stream that featured the very expensive cars utilised by an overwhelmingly rich populace. The crowded streets were lined with elegant exclusive stores. Even at first glance the Mediterranean city seemed glossier and brighter than others because there was no litter and the buildings all appeared to be in excellent repair.

'Oh, there's the cathedral where we'll be enjoying your big day!' Liz commented excitedly as the limo passed through a large, charming square dominated by the tall trees that framed the weathered cathedral, which was centuries old.

Gaby had indeed done her homework on the history of Themos and the ruling family, her retentive brain having absorbed every fact she'd dug up on the Internet. She had also studied numerous photos of Angel's parents. She had been startled by how much Alexios and Angel both resembled Angel's mother. Alexios had her distinctive black curls and green eyes while Angel had inherited her movie-star perfect features.

Angel came from an exotic background of almost unimaginable wealth, privilege and antiquity. Over the centuries, many larger than life personalities had graced the Diamandis family tree. Womanisers, warriors and adventurers featured heavily in Angel's ancestry. For goodness' sake, she thought ruefully, his mother had been an Arabian princess, a woman so flawlessly beautiful that Gaby had found herself studying her photos in fascination. The story recounted on the official royal website had gently hinted that family opposition had forced the Princess and Angel's father to run away together, and it had all sounded terribly romantic, which did nothing whatsoever to explain Angel's deep cynicism about women and life in general. When Angel had pressed her to marry him, he had, possibly without meaning to, revealed that his own childhood might have been less than perfect, and Gaby was very curious to know that story.

The Aikaterina palace was on the coast outside Leveus. It sat at the centre of a fabulous country estate comprising hundreds of acres of historic gardens and woods that were open to the public on certain days of the year. The woods ran all the way down to a private beach. Gaby had studied pictures online, reading about the original medieval fortress at the core of the building, the Renaissance wings and the Versailles-influenced extension that housed public rooms with a spectacular décor. Money, it seemed, had never been in short supply in the royal family.

'My word...' Liz sighed in wonder as the car swept between giant gilded gates and proceeded at a stately pace along a gravelled driveway lined with graceful cypress trees. Swathes of lush green grass rejoiced in the sun-dappled shade. 'This is some place.'

'It's really beautiful... I'm seeing my dream woodland garden,' Gaby remarked shakily, her nervous tension beginning to climb.

'Dream house, dream life, dream—'

'Angel may be rich as Midas and *look* like a dream, but he's a darned sight more complicated than that!' Liz reminded her twin wryly.

Very sexually driven though, Gaby was thinking helplessly, recalling that heart-stopping clinch against the wall, her body involuntarily tightening deep down inside. She was remembering Angel's assurance that they would have a normal marriage and she marvelled at the concept, convinced as she was that Angel had never enjoyed a normal relationship with a woman in his entire adult life. Women were merely the entertainment in Angel's high-powered unscrupulous world, not equals, never partners. How would he adapt to living with a normal woman with ideas and opinions of her own? Particularly a woman whom he had ruthlessly blackmailed and intimidated into marrying him and who was still as angry as hell over the fact? Well, he would just have to learn, she reasoned with a spirited toss of her bright head as she climbed out of the limo inside the imposing porticoed shelter of the palace entrance and turned back to detach her son from his car seat.

No sooner had she released Alexios's belt than a hand touched her shoulder and she turned round to find Angel impossibly close. 'Let me...' he urged.

Colliding with hawklike dark golden eyes sent the butterflies tumbling through her and an intoxicating wave of awareness claimed her simultaneously, muscles tightening, heart accelerating, nerve endings awakening. On weak legs she stepped back and watched as Angel scooped Alexios out. Her son recognised him and laughed, delighted to see his father again because Angel, who had played with him, signified fun.

'Welcome to your new home,' Angel husked, radiating satisfaction and triumph in one fierce charismatic smile as she accompanied him into a vast marble and gilded entrance hall where several small groups of people awaited them. 'Allow me to introduce you to everyone...'

The first candidate was Marina, a smiling older woman introduced as 'Head of the Nursery'.

Taken aback and not in a good way, Gaby turned to Angel. 'I don't think—'

'Naturally you will be our son's primary carer but there will be occasions, such as the wedding and various events, when we will not be available, and we need a good support system. The nursery staff under Marina's steady hand will step in to fill the gaps.'

Gaby swallowed hard at that blunt appraisal of the near future. She also felt horribly like kicking Angel as though she were a cross and frustrated child. Why did he never discuss things in advance with her? Why did he never warn her? She was *not* unreasonable. He thought of everything but neglected to share his thoughts with her. That was unnerving. She smiled and shook hands with the older woman.

'You needn't worry about the quality of our son's care. Marina was a nursery maid when I was boy. She's kind and affectionate,' Angel murmured in her ear as he led her forward to meet the older man, Dmitri, who ran the household. He brought forward various advisors and administrative staff and, in the midst of those introductions, Gaby was unpleasantly surprised to spot Cassia Romano standing to one side chatting to Liz and Laurie. The slender blonde beauty, who rarely revealed any sort of emotion, wore a surprisingly bright smile. Gaby could see that her friends were disconcerted by that transformation because at university Cassia had not deigned to acknowledge either twin, even though both women had shared classes with her.

'Cassia has volunteered to show you the ropes around here,' Angel informed her calmly. 'She knows how everything works and I believe she has entertainment organised for you and your friends this evening.'

'Does she work for you?' Gaby enquired stiffly.

'Yes. Her father is a senior courtier and I've known her since we were children. It's not easy to define her position because she falls somewhere between an employee and a friend,' Angel advanced. 'And she may not have been very approachable when you first met her, but that will have changed because you are now the future consort.'

'I see.' Gaby did see and she didn't like the news that Cassia still held the status of a trusted friend.

Her reading of Cassia in the past had been that, in spite of constantly playing the 'good friend' card, Cassia would do and say anything to frighten off other women and catch Angel for herself. Even so, Gaby had never seen the smallest sign of intimacy on his part with the beautiful blonde and back then Angel had been very much prone to treating Cassia like the wallpaper, pleasant to have in the room but worthy of no particular notice. And nobody knew better than Gaby that when Angel wanted a woman, he smouldered and burned like the heart of a fire around her, she acknowledged as she encountered a scorching glance from his stunning dark golden eyes and her entire skin surface prickled.

Cassia moved forward. 'I hope your flight wasn't too tiring, Miss Knox,' she murmured with a pleasant smile.

'Gabriella, please. How are you, Cassia?' Gaby asked politely.

'I can't address you by your first name. It would break protocol,' Cassia informed her with deadly seriousness, as if the bending of one little rule would invoke a lightning strike. 'Let me show you to your suite.'

'Thank you, Cassia. I'll take care of that,' Angel interposed, still hugging Alexios to his broad chest like a solid little comforter. Her son was resting his head down sleepily on his father's shoulder, eyelashes drooping.

Angel showed her into a lift tucked in below the sweeping staircase. 'The nursery is on the top floor. I think we'll go there first.'

'Yes, Alexios is tired. He gets all excited about new places and new people and he hasn't slept today.'

Her breath locked in her throat as she looked at him, ensnared by black-lashed tawny eyes that she could not withstand, and it was like standing too close to a fire, getting burned but still craving the pain.

'Theos mou...' Angel growled in a roughened undertone. 'I want you.'

Every nerve ending in Gaby's body melted into liquidity and overheated her. She was frozen there, her brain momentarily in stasis from the sheer rush of excitement. Angel closed the distance between them, pressing her back against the wall of the lift while his mouth hungrily crashed down on hers. His tongue delved between her parted lips and she was electrified, desire like a roaring wave engulfing her trembling body. Her hand flew up, fingers splaying to spear into his hair and hold him to her. He ravished her mouth with feverish urgency, his passion unleashed, and she was utterly lost in the sensation and excitement of the moment when a little squeak of protest alerted her to the reality that Alexios was being squashed between their bodies.

She jerked sideways and back from Angel as though she had been burned by a live wire and, in a way, she felt as though she had been.

Angel stared down at her in consternation. He had not intended to touch her, but no woman made him feel what Gabriella made him feel: that agonising, clawing need to physically connect. He didn't want that kind of incendiary bond with *any* woman, he never had because he knew the pitfalls all too well. Hadn't he watched his father sink into the gutter in his attempt to hold his own with the woman he had married, the woman he'd loved beyond reason?

'I don't think that was a very good idea,' Gaby quipped, controlling her anger at both him and herself with difficulty as she lifted her complaining son out of his arms.

'It was exactly what I wanted. Celibacy doesn't agree with me,' Angel imparted as they stepped out of the lift. 'I'll be in your room when you return from your evening out.'

Gaby flushed to the roots of her hair, thinking guiltily that he could hardly be blamed for the assumption that he would be welcome in her bed, and she squashed the instant leap of excitement at that idea. She was annoyed that she had not pushed him away. Why did she always let herself down around Angel? Why could she never deny the irresistible pull he exerted over her? Just for once, couldn't she have stepped back and told him tartly to keep his distance?

'No, please don't bother,' she warned him. 'I think you're forgetting how low you had to sink to get me to agree to this marriage.'

'No, that *wasn't* me sinking low. I believe that I was aiming *high*! Admittedly I put you under pressure, but I was thinking of the future and taking a unilateral decision as to what was best for the three of us as a family,' Angel shot back at her without apology. In fact, he had the nerve to give her a questioning look as though astonished that she had not yet recognised the higher purpose behind his intimidation tactics.

Gaby gritted her teeth, reckoning that he was shrewd enough to have justified anything short of murder. 'I should've known you'd behave as though you did us all a favour!' she snapped.

'So, you're pulling a Lysistrata to punish me…you're on a sex strike,' Angel clarified very drily, referring to the ancient Greek comedy by Aristophanes. 'And how good a start do you think that will give our marriage?'

'Right at this moment, I don't really care!' Gaby told him truthfully as he led the way into a very grand nursery that was startlingly contemporary.

'I had it updated for Alexios. It hadn't been used since I was a little boy,' he explained when he saw her staring at the very fancy train-shaped cot and the purpose-built storage for toys and books, every shelf already packed in readiness with items calculated to appeal to a toddler.

Marina appeared with Alexios's shabby baby bag in tow, and Gaby's rigid stance eased and she smiled in relief. In a matter of minutes, Alexios was changed and tucked into the cot. Angel closed a hand over her stiff fingers and led her away again. 'Cassia has some kind of hen party organised for you tonight, but I imagine that it will be a very *proper* event, shorn of phallic symbols and any silliness. She's invited my uncle, Prince Timon's two daughters.'

'Your cousins, who are acting as bridesmaids for us?' Gaby broke in.

'Yes, and some other young relatives whom you should meet before the wedding.'

Gaby nodded. 'Where are you heading tonight?'

'To a business investment dinner,' Angel

told her, urging her down another flight of stairs. 'Generally, I have a pretty packed calendar, but I've pushed as much as I can to later in the season to enable me to spend time with you and Alexios.'

'We shall be honoured,' Gaby responded deadpan, only to still as Cassia emerged from a room just ahead of them.

'Forgive me for interrupting you but the Crown council meeting is about to begin downstairs, sir,' she announced. 'I can show your fiancée to her room.'

'If you will excuse me,' Angel murmured, stepping away from Gaby.

'Come this way, Miss Knox,' Cassia directed with confidence.

Gaby compressed her lips because she had wanted to tackle Angel about the nursery being a ten-minute hike from her room and Cassia's company was unlikely to ever be welcome. On the other hand, had she stayed with Angel in the mood she was in, they would probably have had another argument, she acknowledged ruefully. Perhaps she should be grateful for a breathing space.

'These are your rooms,' Cassia announced, throwing wide the door of a large sitting room and standing back for Gaby to precede her over the threshold. 'Last occupied by the Prince's mother and freshly decorated for you.'

The décor was very grand in airy shades of white, pale blue and green. Delicate panels painted with classic flowers ornamented the walls, providing the perfect backdrop for the beautifully crafted modern furniture. A huge bunch of artistically arranged flowers in a crystal vase scented the air. Cassia opened doors to show her the bedroom, the adjoining bathroom and the dressing room, saying, 'I hope you like the clothes...'

'Clothes?' Gaby queried with a frown.

Cassia slid back some doors to display a multitude of garments hung in zipped bags and entire shelves of folded clothing. 'The Prince ordered a new wardrobe for you.'

'That was very generous of him but I shan't *need* all this,' Gaby said.

'Living on Themos, you will need all of it. Wearing designer apparel is part of your public image as the ruler's wife,' Cassia informed her. 'I would suggest you choose a cocktail dress for dining out tonight. I hired a maid with the experience to do your hair and advise you on outfits.'

Gaby pushed a polite smile onto her lips. 'How thoughtful of you,' she said quietly.

'In the circumstances, I'm being very generous,' the blonde told her disquietingly.

'Which circumstances would those be?' Gaby asked.

Cassia folded her rather thin lips. 'Your bridegroom was originally planning to marry me... Oh, the Prince never said so, but I *knew* that he saw me as an ideal match.'

'Good heavens...' Gaby muttered in a shaken undertone. 'I had no idea.'

'Why should you have?' Cassia responded dismissively. 'That's water under the bridge now...forget I mentioned it.'

'Yes,' Gaby agreed, grateful to move on from an awkward subject but thoroughly needled by the blonde's coy little announcement. It stung, made her feel like a usurper in the position that Angel had given her. Cassia just oozed smugness and conceit. But was her contention true? How could the blonde beauty make such a claim when even she admitted that Angel had never discussed the subject with her? Of course, Cassia enjoyed unlimited confidence.

And Gaby could quite see that, as a local, accustomed to the royal lifestyle by her father's standing, Cassia Romano, with her icy aristocratic elegance and perfect diction, would have been an excellent choice of bride for Angel. Only the fact that Angel had never actually got around to mentioning marriage to Cassia or even reviewing the idea with her struck Gaby as revealing, much more revealing than Cassia was willing to accept. In reality, Angel had been in no hurry to marry anyone and only their son's accidental arrival had changed that.

'Your friends are in the suite opposite,' Cassia told her as she departed. 'We'll be leaving for dinner at seven.'

Liz, who was a real fashion buff, had a ball trawling through Gaby's new collection of clothing. Both women were shell-shocked when she shared Cassia's announcement.

'I know,' Gaby groaned. 'I didn't know how to feel about her saying that either.'

'Perhaps she's simply a very honest person and preferred to put the fact out there,' Liz opined with a wince.

'Maybe it was all in her head, this idea that Angel was planning to marry her, and she just likes to play the victim.' Laurie was less charitable. 'I can see no good reason for her to share her personal belief that she was to be his wife with anyone...particularly with the woman he's about to marry.'

'I think possibly Cassia may just be a little strange.' Gaby sighed, fingering a silky blue dress that appealed to her and tugging out a strappy pair of blue pearlised sandals that she couldn't wait to try on. She would not complain to Angel about the new clothes he had provided because her own wardrobe contained very few fancy outfits and none at all that could have qualified as designer. 'I think I'll wear this…it's smart without being over the top.'

'Do you think we'll be heading to a night-club after the meal?' Laurie asked wistfully.

Gaby grimaced. 'I doubt it. Cassia doesn't strike me as the type, but look on the bright side…eating out is infinitely preferable to a formal reception staged simply for people to meet the bride.'

An hour later, fully dressed and ready to join her friends, Gaby emerged from her bed-room and came to a halt when she found Angel awaiting her in the sitting room. He was poised by the window, sunshine gleam-ing over his black hair, accentuating his hard, bronzed features and the sharp edges and hol-lows that made him so strikingly handsome.

'I forgot to give you this,' he murmured, stalking forward and reaching for her hand. Without hesitation he threaded a giant square-cut sapphire and diamond ring on her wedding finger. 'Everyone will be expecting to see a ring…why disappoint them?'

Gabriella looked fabulous in an understated dress that made the most of her feminine curves and slender shapely legs. The colour brought out the blueness of her eyes, the porcelain fairness of her skin and intensified the copper vibrance of her tumbling hair.

'Oh, I don't know…' Gaby stretched out a hand to watch the gorgeous jewels glitter in the sunlight. The sapphire was a deep velvety blue, surrounded by tapered baguette diamonds in a ballerina setting. She was shaken by its sheer *presence* on her finger. It was the sort of a ring that would stop traffic in the street, and she struggled to act as though she were accustomed to such magnificence. 'Is it really necessary to fake an engagement?'

Angel frowned, black brows pleating. There were times when Gabriella frustrated him beyond belief, and this was one of them. He didn't understand her in the way he had long understood other women. She didn't go into ecstasies over expensive jewellery, and she hadn't even mentioned the clothes. The gestures that usually smoothed feminine pride and other sensitivities didn't work for him with her.

'I meant well,' he breathed tautly. 'It's hardly fake when we're getting married the day after tomorrow, is it? But we skipped the conventional steps.'

'We skipped a lot of stuff,' Gaby told him tightly.

Intoxicating dark golden eyes framed by lush black lashes held hers. 'But this is a fresh start.'

'No, it's another chapter. We didn't *have* a proper start so we can scarcely have a fresh one,' Gaby contradicted, her tension easing only when her friends appeared in the doorway. 'Sorry, I have to go.'

All the way down to the entrance hall where Cassia awaited their arrival, Gaby castigated herself for her ungracious behaviour with Angel. She dug out her phone and texted him straight away, telling him how much she loved the ring and she thanked him very much for the new clothes. Sometimes in an effort to play it cool with Angel, she got things badly wrong and slid into sulky ingratitude, she acknowledged uneasily as her friends exclaimed in wonderment over the glittering sapphire and Cassia's lips flattened to a thin line on her words of congratulation.

The restaurant was very large and imposing and frantically busy. Gaby thought it was a surprising venue in which to stage a small, supposedly discreet dinner party. They were met at the door and conveyed straight to a central circular table. Several other young women were already seated there. In the flurry of bright introductions that followed and the serving of drinks, Gaby's tension began to lift. She sipped the glass of champagne that was served to her first, noticing that Cassia seemed to intimidate the other women present, giving her the impression that the blonde was not widely liked.

Not long after she had ordered her meal, she began to feel very hot. 'Are you warm?' she asked Liz.

'No, I'm fine. The food looks amazing,' her friend confided. 'But I'm surprised Cassia decided to stage this somewhere so public. Every diner here is frantically trying to work out which of us is Angel's bride and I've seen people taking covert photos on their phones.'

Gaby struggled to focus on Liz's amused face. Her mouth was very dry, and the room felt airless. As her tummy gave a nauseous lurch that terrified her, she flew upright. 'I'm off to the cloakroom.'

'Want company?'

'No, no, thanks.' Gaby didn't want an audience if she was about to be ill, nor did she wish to cast a dampener on the evening out. As she straightened, she felt dizzy and she wondered if she had picked up some ghastly bug travelling. Well, she would just have to get over it and fast, she thought worriedly as she followed the sign into a plush cloakroom. Her legs felt weak. Her breath rattled in her chest and something akin to panic assailed her at the rapidity with which she was falling ill. She dug out her phone and, without even thinking about it, pressed Angel's number.

'I'm not well,' she whispered. 'I'm feeling really ill, Angel…don't want to wreck the party—'

'Where are you?'

'Don't know name of restaurant…in the cloakroom,' she slurred as she slumped down on a padded chair.

The claustrophobic room was swirling round her, and the phone slid from her fingers as her head fell back, too heavy for her to hold upright. A moment later, she knew no more.

CHAPTER SEVEN

GABY WAKENED GROGGILY in a darkened room, snatches of foggy recollection tugging at her woozy brain. Her lashes fluttered in confusion as she slowly breathed in and out, relieved to discover that she could catch her breath easily again. She shifted her arm, and something tugged painfully at her skin, causing a sound of discomfort to escape her.

A hand settled over hers. 'Relax. You have an IV line in...you were dehydrated,' Angel explained.

And the instant she heard his voice, Gaby felt the panic recede and she was soothed. She remembered the tightness in her chest, the difficulty in breathing and the way she had slumped in the cloakroom. 'I'm sorry,' she mumbled, taking in her surroundings and realising that hours must have passed because it was dark beyond the window. 'What time is it?'

'It's the middle of the night. You weren't fully unconscious when I found you, but this is the first time you've come round enough to speak,' Angel told her grimly.

'I'm in hospital?'

'Yes, but I'm taking you out of here the minute the doctor tells me I can,' Angel announced as he paced at the foot of the bed.

He looked ruffled, black hair tousled, his tie loosened, dark stubble outlining his strong jaw line. He still looked gorgeous though, just a little less immaculate than usual. 'I felt ill… I phoned you,' she recalled thickly, trying to regroup and compose herself.

'And I thank God that you did,' Angel breathed with raw sincerity. 'You were roofied…in a public restaurant. It is beyond belief that such a thing could happen to my bride! I could not believe that you could be at risk of any kind on such an outing. Believe me, I will not be so careless of your safety again!'

'Roofied?' Gaby gasped in disbelief. 'I was drugged? How is that possible?'

'We will find out,' Angel intoned wrathfully, smouldering golden eyes welded to the pale drawn triangle of her face. 'I assure you that we will find out who is responsible for this outrage. But it makes no sense. It is not as though you were in a club where someone might hope to steal you away from your companions. Nowhere could have been more public, more apparently safe…the police want you to make a statement.'

Gaby was reeling from what he had told her. 'Of course—'

'Like me, they are very much taken aback by this assault and are determined to find the culprit,' Angel breathed heavily. 'I would never have forgiven myself had anything happened to you. Why on earth did you leave the table?'

'I wasn't feeling well, and I didn't want to spoil the evening for everybody. I thought if I got away I would get some air and start feeling better…but when I think about it, that was foolish.'

'Yes. It was dangerous, less safe for you to do that…but in a crowded restaurant and with you the guest of honour, who could have hoped to have removed you from the premises without it being noticed?'

'Maybe that wasn't the intent, maybe someone just wanted to make me ill,' Gaby muttered uncertainly. 'I only had one glass of champagne and nothing to eat. We had only just ordered. The only people who came close to me were the sommelier and the waiter.'

'Unless the drug was administered by one

of your companions at the table,' Angel slotted in darkly. 'We cannot ignore that possibility, unpleasant though it is to suspect friends and family members of such an offence.'

'*Not* Liz and Laurie,' Gaby affirmed her complete trust in her friends.

A doctor arrived to check her over. Angel hovered, his anxiety a revelation to her because she had never seen Angel less than cool and collected or so concerned about anything. She was shaken too by the acceptance that when she had begun to panic as her body had failed to cooperate with her, she had instinctively turned to him for help. Without a moment's hesitation she had known that she could depend on him in a crisis and that revealed a level of basic trust in Angel that she had not known she had.

'Liz and Laurie are waiting outside to see you. They couldn't be persuaded to continue the evening and they followed me to the hospital in a taxi,' he told her with faint amusement. 'Despite my discouragement.'

'Never try to come between a woman and her best friends,' Gaby teased with a sudden smile.

A wicked grin of amusement chased the gravity from Angel's firm, sensual mouth and his dark golden eyes smouldered a lighter shade. Her mouth ran dry as her nipples pinched taut and an almost unbearable ache stirred between her thighs. Hunger clawed at her and she gritted her teeth in an effort to restrain that fierce surge of sexual awareness. As colour washed her cheeks, she turned her head away in embarrassment. 'I still can't believe that someone gave me a drug... I suppose I don't *want* to believe it.'

'None of us do but you arrived here quickly enough for the hospital to administer a blood test and we have the proof.' Angel sank down on the edge of the bed, dangerously close, frustratingly far, the faint scent of his cologne assailing her, achingly familiar. 'From this moment on you will enjoy a steel ring of protection around you...*nothing* like this will ever happen to you on my watch again,' he swore emphatically.

'It's not your fault. There are people who do bad stuff everywhere,' Gaby whispered soothingly, touched by his desire to make her feel safe again and ashamed of her own responses.

She had wanted to drag him down into the bed with her and the intensity of that desire shocked her. Attraction was one thing, ferocious craving an unbalanced and obsessive response, and Gaby admired restraint and sense much more. She could not admire the needy woman whom Angel was turning her into. It took her back to university and the pain of severance when Angel had finished his exams and returned to Themos. She had believed that she would never see him again and while in one way it had been a relief, in another it had hurt intolerably. Not for anyone was she revisiting those feelings, she assured herself bracingly.

She gave a statement to a police inspector who was very nervous at being in Angel's presence. Gaby had nothing much to tell the officer. She had not noticed anyone paying particular attention to her in the restaurant and did not feel that she made a very good witness. Liz and Laurie came in to visit her and Liz admitted that she had suspected something was wrong and had followed her to the cloakroom, only to find her passed out.

'And then Angel arrived when I was trying to revive you and it was all high drama then. He was very upset, and he grabbed you up and carried you out of the rear entrance of the restaurant with all his security men trying to take you off him and he wasn't having that. He didn't want anyone else touching you.'

'You know, I've never been his biggest fan,' Laurie chipped in ruefully. 'But he *is* brilliant in an emergency. I saw another side to him.

He's very protective and he was in a rage that you had been harmed but his temper didn't get in the way of ensuring that you received immediate attention.'

At some stage of their visit, Gaby drifted into a doze and when she wakened again, Angel was back with her and a golden dawn was lifting the light levels in the room. 'Have you been here all night?' she asked, noting that the stubble surrounding his wide, sensual mouth was much darker and heavier.

'Yes. The doctors are happy for you to leave now and your maid has sent a change of clothes for you. If you feel up to it, we'll head back to the palace for breakfast.'

Uncomfortable because she felt such a mess, Gaby sat up and pushed back the sheet to swing her legs experimentally off the side of the bed.

'Careful,' Angel warned, cupping her elbow to keep her steady. 'You could still be dizzy.'

Gaby grasped the bag he handed her and entered the bathroom, keen to remove her make-up and have a shower. Her reflection made her groan out loud. Her eye make-up had smudged, and she looked like a racoon. The shower refreshed her, but she still felt uncharacteristically weak. Not the way a woman wanted to feel the day before her wedding, she reflected ruefully, wondering who on earth had put that drug in her drink. Or even had it been meant for someone else at the table? Mulling over every possible permutation of what had happened, she put on the tailored trousers and top packed for her use and brushed her messy hair before bundling it up in a bun.

'I think I'll need another nap,' she confided in the limousine wafting them back to the palace. 'But Alexios will be wondering where I am.'

'When we get back, I'll spend some time with him. You need to rest. The wedding will be tiring,' Angel warned her. 'And I have some jewellery for you to examine.'

Back at the palace, Gaby took a nap. When she was up again, Angel brought a collection of jewellery to her suite and encouraged her to look at the pieces. 'I am hoping that you will choose to wear the sapphire set with your wedding dress. They are family heirlooms.'

Shock having seized hold of her lungs, Gaby stared down in disbelief at the jewellery on display for her benefit. It comprised a magnificent sapphire and diamond tiara, a pendant and earrings. 'Wow,' she framed limply, for she had no words to describe such glittering theatrical opulence. 'Did this superb set belong to your mother?'

'No, my mother preferred contemporary pieces. The sapphire set belonged to my father's mother. They are of Russian origin and design and she brought them with her when she married my grandfather. The choice of whether or not you wear them tomorrow is, of course, yours.' Angel paused. 'I believe you have a dress fitting now...your maid reminded me.'

Gaby winced. 'I forgot about that!'

'They're waiting for you in the room across the corridor,' Angel told her helpfully.

The afternoon bled away in a welter of wedding business, from how she was to wear her hair to which door she was to use entering the cathedral. A miniature map of the floorplan was laid in front of her. Not having realised until that point quite how elaborate the arrangements had to be for so large and important a wedding, Gaby began feeling increasingly nervous. What would Angel expect of her in her role as his consort? Would she be able to cope? As anxious as she was, it was a relief to head up to the nursery where she planned to spend some time with her son.

Alexios, however, was in the bath and when she peered in, she was taken aback by the sight of Angel in his shirtsleeves getting thoroughly wet as he divebombed their son's plastic ducks from on high. Water splashed everywhere as Alexios squealed with pleasure and smacked the water in excitement.

Marina, hovering at the back of the room holding Angel's jacket, beamed and stepped back into the nursery to join Gaby. 'They are having so much fun together,' she said happily.

'Yes,' Gaby agreed. 'I won't disturb them. I'll come back to feed Alexios in half an hour.'

In truth she was fascinated to see Angel more relaxed than she had ever seen him, his luxuriant black hair tousled, dense black lashes low over glittering dark eyes narrowed with mirth and appreciation, his damp shirt plastered to the sculpted lines of his muscular chest.

And she thought then, *this* is what he meant about being a 'normal' family, this is what Angel wants for our son and what he will actively strive to create. For the very first time, Gaby fully accepted that Alexios was Angel's son as well and she was grateful for their connection. In fact, she was impressed that Angel was putting in the effort and not simply going through the motions or relying on his wealth and what he could buy for his son's entertainment to do that bonding for him. Alexios was acquiring a father with an old-fashioned hands-on approach and she could not have been happier for her son. If only she didn't have to wonder if she would receive the same keen attention as Angel's wife…but she didn't want to be a duty in Angel's life or an extension of her son in his eyes. She was winding herself up, agonising about what he felt, and she felt, she told herself irritably. Where was the profit in that?

'So, nerves eating you alive yet?' Liz teased when the three women gathered for a relaxed spa evening in Gaby's sitting room.

'They will be by tomorrow but right now…' Gaby lifted her hands and dropped them again '… I have no regrets and I'm convinced that I've made the right decision.'

CHAPTER EIGHT

GABY TOOK A final spin in front of the cheval mirror and the silk crepe skirt overlaid with Italian silk studded with crystals and mother-of-pearl teardrops flared out with the sleek weight of a luxury finish round her legs.

The off-the-shoulder design and skilled shaping at waist and hip flattered her curves while the narrow column of the skirt and her high heels gave her extra height. With the fabulous tiara anchored like a coronet of diamond fire in her mass of upswept copper hair, and the sapphire earrings and matching pendant, she knew that she had never looked better, and that knowledge gave her much-needed confidence.

'Absolutely fantastic,' Liz sighed fondly, snapping yet another photo with her phone.

'Are you ready, ladies?' Cassia asked brightly from the doorway. 'Could I have a private word with the bride before we leave for the cere-mony?'

Liz walked straight out but Laurie walked across to the dressing table and fluffed her hair, taking her time over departing. Cassia, sheathed in a stylish cinnamon-coloured dress looked as glossy and bandbox fresh as if she had stepped straight off a magazine cover. She closed the door to ensure the conversation could not be overheard and Gaby's brow furrowed, her tension suddenly increasing.

'Cassia?' she questioned uneasily.

'I've agonised long and hard over whether or not to tell you about my personal relationship with Angel,' the blonde told her calmly. 'But, going forward, I prefer to be honest and open…'

'I haven't a clue what you're talking about,' Gaby admitted in a strained undertone.

'Angel and I have been lovers for years and I don't expect that to change after the wedding,' Cassia murmured, her face flushed, her pale eyes cast modestly down. 'We have a long-term, convenient connection. You will have to accept that if you want your marriage to work. Angel expects to do as he likes when he likes and that will not change.'

Gaby's chin lifted, her eyes cool as Cassia's drawling tone of self-satisfaction sent ice splinters travelling through her tummy. 'I don't believe you,' she retorted flatly.

She knew Angel better than she had years earlier and she recognised his essential streak of honour and decency, which was also laced with honesty. She doubted very much that Angel was indulging in some grubby sexual relationship with an employee behind closed doors.

That bold proclamation of disbelief seemed to disconcert the other woman. Cassia straightened her shoulders, her pale blue eyes sharp and glassy with the sheer loathing she had previously worked so hard to hide but which now shone like a beacon in her gaze. 'I assure you that I am telling you the truth. For goodness' sake, why on earth would I lie to you about such a thing?'

Gaby resisted a powerful urge to enlighten Cassia about the effects of jealousy, rage and resentment on the female psyche. Cassia had patiently waited for her moment backstage for years while Angel entertained himself with an endless variety of women. Possibly, Cassia had assumed that age and boredom would make Angel switch his focus to matrimony and finally acknowledge that his reliable friend and right-hand woman, Cassia, would make the perfect wife. But, sadly for her, it hadn't happened. Not only had Angel failed to demonstrate any pressing need to settle down, but he had also fathered a son who could not be ignored with another woman. And all of a sudden, Cassia had found herself out in the cold, serving a rival whom she viewed as vastly inferior to her superior self.

'You're lying,' Gaby stated with quiet conviction. 'I understand why and I'm sorry that you feel the way that you obviously do, but there is nothing anyone can do to change the situation and I fully intend to marry Angel today.'

'You'll regret this!' Cassia hissed in a seething undertone. 'Believe me, you'll regret it! I'll make your life hell and don't doubt that I have the power to do it!'

All that Gaby regretted at that moment was the knowledge that she would have to share their conversation with Angel. How could she possibly work with or accept advice from a woman who hated her? She wasn't looking forward to having to explain why that was so to Angel, who would not be happy because he had long regarded Cassia as a dependable friend.

* * *

'And you really don't think that there's a shred of truth to her story?' Laurie prompted her friend worriedly fifteen minutes later during their drive to the cathedral.

Gaby's dark blue eyes were calm. 'I don't. I'm a good observer and I've never seen even a hint of physical familiarity or sexual awareness between them. It was Cassia's last-ditch attempt to wreck the wedding but, unfortunately for her, it didn't work.'

Liz was frowning. 'I can't see Angel having an affair with a member of his staff…and why would he want to anyway? He's never been short of female attention. You'll have to tell him what she said.'

Gaby winced. 'Some time obviously but not today. I'm not going to let Cassia get to me.'

Laurie smiled. 'That's the right attitude to have. But just the same, I'll send you the recording.'

Gaby's eyes widened. '*Recording?* What recording?'

'I don't trust Cassia. I left my phone on the dressing table in the bedroom to record your conversation before I left you alone with her,' she confided.

'My word, my sister, the consummate spy!' Liz gasped in delight.

'You recorded us?' Gaby prompted in astonishment as her friend simply nodded and grimaced.

'Sorry, I just didn't trust her at all...'

Walking down the aisle in the echoing grandeur of the cathedral with its soaring ceilings and packed pews demanded every bit of Gaby's confidence. She worked at keeping her head high, looking neither left nor right even as she felt the rustle of turning heads and heard the low murmur of comment that accompanied her passage. Angel wanted her to be his wife. That knowledge lifted her. It was only that the packed cathedral and her new status were a little intimidating. At the altar she saw Angel with another equally tall black-haired man by his side and she saw Angel swing round to openly stare as she approached, and colour flared like a burning banner in her cheeks.

One look at his bride and Angel was riveted to the spot. Gabriella's dress clung lovingly to her shapely curves and yet exposed only her creamy shoulders. Her glorious hair was piled in a vibrant copper mass on top of her head, providing a wonderful setting for the superb tiara glittering below the lights. The priceless sapphires merely enhanced her bright blue eyes and the luminosity of her skin.

'I'm impressed, little brother,' Crown Prince Saif of Alharia murmured softly from behind him. 'You did better than well.'

Angel's calm soothed Gaby's galloping nerves. They might have been alone in the room for all the attention he paid to their surroundings and their audience. She supposed that level of sangfroid only came with practice and experience. During the ceremony, he lifted her hand to slide on the platinum wedding ring and she glanced up, ensnared by his stunning tigerish eyes, and her heart started to race in spite of the acid reminders she was pushing quite deliberately through her brain.

This was the guy who had blackmailed her to the altar and trapped her between a rock and a hard place by using her precious son as a weapon against her. And he might have tried to wrap up his behaviour in clean linen by insisting that he was only thinking of what was best for all three of them but, in truth, Angel had merely utilised his power to get what he wanted at speed and with minimal personal effort. And he hadn't given her any time at all to adjust to the new status quo. Worse still, his demand for 'normal' in such an abnormal marriage was even less reasonable.

Desperately stoking up her anger in self-defence, she listened while the priest spoke timeless words over their bent heads. She looked at the ring on her hand and contemplated a truth she had long avoided. She had been in love with Angel at university, but she had refused to admit it to herself. In those days, unhappily, she had underestimated Angel's stubborn, wilful streak. She had assumed that he would compromise over the NDA she had refused to sign. She had failed to recognise just how ruthless Angel was at heart, not to mention how swiftly he would move on from her. The hurt inflicted by that rejection had taught her not to assume that a man would react the same way she did to obstacles. Angel hadn't cared enough about her to reconsider his boundaries or his rules. Indeed, when she had coincidentally seen him kissing that other woman at the party, he had been demonstrating his indifference to her...and hitting back. Don't forget that, she reminded herself doggedly. Angel was a vengeful soul.

Indeed, so fiercely and efficiently did Gaby revive her every worst thought and feeling about Angel that her profile might have been chipped out of pure ice as they walked back down the aisle again, his arm resting lightly at the base of her rigid spine. Only at that point did she register that she was reviving her negative outlook as a defence against the other powerful emotions flooding her. Angel and what he might do and what he thought meant so much to her *because* she still *loved* him.

It was a moment of revelation that shook and stunned Gaby in the wake of that anxious flood of critical recollections. Fear of allowing Angel to have that power over her again had made her throw up every possible barrier because naturally she didn't want to get hurt again. Only, sadly, her emotions and the world in general were not under her control.

'You look stunning,' Angel murmured softly. 'But you can smile now.'

'To do that I would have to have something to smile about,' Gaby countered in a dry joke, her mouth quirking as they walked out onto the steps, and dismay gripped her when she realised that television cameras awaited them.

Angel caught both her hands in his and tugged her round to face at him. 'We did it for Alexios but that doesn't mean that we can't enjoy being together,' he told her softly, his dark drawl roughening as he gazed down at her. 'Or that we can't make a huge success of this marriage.'

His striking dark golden eyes held hers with savage intensity, as though he were demanding that she concede those points. A flush of heat and awareness enveloped her entire body, slowly sliding over her prickling skin like a silken caress, awakening every nerve ending and causing a tightening at her feminine core. The sensation was so strong that it almost hurt, and the tip of her tongue slid out to wet her taut lower lip.

'Don't do that when we're in public,' Angel warned her in a roughened sensual undertone. 'It turns me on way too much.'

Gaby's eyes widened and the butterflies tumbled in her stomach and for the space of ten seconds there was nothing and nobody else in the world for her. He linked his fingers with hers and walked her down the steps past the flashing cameras and shouted congratulations. She was still trying to catch her breath as he tucked her into the waiting limousine.

'I'm looking forward to introducing you to my brother, Saif, and his wife, Tatiana, at the reception,' Angel volunteered with a shimmering smile.

'You have a brother?' Gaby exclaimed with incredulity, still struggling to shake herself free of the sensual spell that he could cast. 'Since when did *you* have a brother?'

'A half-brother from my mother's first marriage,' he explained. 'My brother is the Crown

Prince of Alharia. Our mother was married to his father, the Emir, first. She deserted the Emir and my baby brother to run off with my father. The divorce was very discreet. I was born only weeks after my parents married.'

'Why was your relationship with your brother kept a secret?' Gaby prompted in curiosity.

'Saif's father is old and ill and still sensitive to that ancient scandal. Saif knew the Emir would be upset if he admitted that he had sought me out, but he finally bit the bullet and owned up. Today he just turned up and told me that he intended to be my best man. I was shocked,' Angel confided with a softened light in his gaze. 'But I was very pleased to have him by my side.'

'I can see you were,' Gaby admitted, jolted by the emotion unhidden in his expressive eyes. 'Oh, my goodness, now I know what you were doing in Alharia when we met again! Obviously, I guessed you were a wedding guest but—'

'Yes, I flew in for Saif's wedding only to discover that I couldn't show my face at the event in case I was recognised. He hadn't told his father about our friendship at that stage,' Angel told her heavily. 'That was a sobering experience...'

Gaby wondered how much experiencing that disappointment that same day, over his brother's reluctance to acknowledge their familial bond, had influenced Angel in his attitude towards her that night when Alexios had been conceived. 'I expect it was…and Saif must have felt it too. I'm sure he must've felt that he was letting you down,' she remarked thoughtfully. 'That's why he was so determined to show up for *your* wedding and show the world that he is your brother and proud of it.'

Angel glanced at her with veiled appreciation, impressed by her understanding. 'He's sensitive that way, more so than me. I did understand how difficult a position he was in, with the Emir having a weak heart. That's why Saif being here today with his wife and son means a great deal to me. Their son, Amir, is almost the same age as Alexios…'

'And our sons will totally ignore each other,' Gaby forecast with a chuckle. 'They're too young to be playmates yet.'

Much of the tension that had gripped her in the cathedral had drained away again. 'So, your mother left Saif behind in Alharia as a baby when she met your father. That must've been a very difficult decision for her to make.'

Angel shot her a wry shuttered glance. 'I

doubt it. She didn't like children much. She never saw Saif again and she didn't *try* to see him either. Saif swears that his father would have allowed her access to him, but she never asked for it. Instead, she acted as though he had never been born.'

In receipt of that rather astonishing information, Gaby widened her eyes, and her lips parted in a soundless 'oh' of surprise. Saying that she *didn't like children much* was a very revealing admission to make about one's mother, she reflected on a surge of frustrated curiosity, but, as the limousine was drawing up at the palace, she clamped her tongue between her teeth and said nothing before gathering herself to walk back into public view.

A photo session had been set up in one of the grand ground-floor reception rooms. The wedding party was the main feature of those photos. She was briefly introduced to Prince Saif, who grinned at her and waved at a small blonde carrying a baby. 'My wife, Tatiana. She's dying to meet you.'

'I shall look forward to it,' Gaby said warmly as Marina appeared in the background with Alexios.

'Do you have any objection to Alexios joining us for the photos?' Angel murmured covertly. 'I thought it would be a pleasant, unfussy way of introducing him to our country.'

'No, I think it's a good idea,' Gaby agreed, flushing as the photographer sent her a reproachful look as he tried to keep everyone engaged with the session. 'But I'd agree to anything right now to get my paws on my son again. I've hardly seen Alexios since we arrived.'

'It looks as though he feels much the same way,' Angel remarked, watching his son squirm frantically in Marina's hold and stretch out desperate arms in his mother's direction.

Gaby clasped her son and endeavoured to restrain him from bouncing on her lap. Angel grabbed him and occupied him for a few minutes. The photo session came to an end. Alexios returned sleepily to Marina, and Angel and Gaby greeted their guests in the ballroom where the meal was being served. She met Saif's wife, Tatiana, and took to her immediately. Her warmth and friendliness were very welcome, and it was no time before the two women and Liz and Laurie were discussing babies and laughing while Alexios and Amir sat on a rug side by side, only noticing each other when the more mobile Alexios moved to snatch at a toy that Amir also had his eye on.

Laurie approached her when they were taking their seats for the meal. 'Have you told Angel yet about Cassia?' she asked covertly. 'I've sent you the recording.'

'Thanks...no, not yet. I'll choose a quieter moment,' Gaby declared, reluctant to admit that she really didn't want to tackle the topic or make use of the recording. It seemed underhand.

In addition, Gaby didn't like attacking or confronting people. Perhaps resentment had sent Cassia recklessly over the edge and she would regret her wild claim and the subject would never be mentioned again. Did she really want to be responsible for Cassia being disgraced and losing her job? Gaby didn't believe that Cassia was Angel's occasional mistress, she really *didn't*...but she supposed there was always the chance that she was being foolishly blind and naive, and she had to share that little scene with Angel.

'So,' Gaby whispered under cover of the music during the meal. 'Are we going anywhere after this ends?'

'Into the mountains to my grandparents' hideaway,' Angel murmured. 'Although we have many other more glamorous options. I have a yacht and property in several major cities, but I thought that right now we would both enjoy time to decompress in a peaceful setting. Alexios and Marina will join us there tomorrow.'

'Oh…'

'You can tuck him in for the night before we leave,' Angel told her teasingly.

Angel's uncle, Prince Timon, and his wife took charge of the reception late afternoon and urged the bride and groom to make a quiet getaway.

'Don't take off the dress,' Angel urged as Gaby walked towards the stairs, intending to do just that.

She spun back, soft pink warming her cheeks. 'I was planning to put on something comfy.'

'That doesn't sound very sexy,' Angel husked. 'And the dress and the sapphires are a dynamite combo.'

'I *can't* travel to a mountain hideaway in a tiara and a wedding dress!' she hissed back half under her breath.

'We have one wedding day, one wedding night…this is a special occasion,' Angel persisted, his dazzling dark golden eyes gripping her. 'Let's for once leave the sensible and the comfortable for another day, *hara mou*.'

'I'm *not* always sensible!' Gaby bit out in a mortified undertone.

His brilliant eyes gleamed. 'If you're not, *prove* it.'

It was true and she wanted to kick him for knowing the fact. She had always been sensible. Her parents had raised her that way, teaching her to set a good example for her little brother. After the death of her family and the pained awareness that her aunt really didn't want the stress of raising a teenager and had only taken her on out of a sense of duty, Gaby had known that she could not afford to make any waves and she had focussed on being even *more* sensible. In denial of the obvious, she climbed into the SUV that awaited them outside the palace still in her dress and the sapphires. With incredulity, she watched Angel swing into the driving seat, sleek and assured in faded jeans and an open shirt.

'*You*…changed,' she enunciated grittily.

'Yes…why? Were you just gasping for the opportunity to strip me out of my morning suit…or were you hoping I would do a lap dance for you and make the encounter a little more stimulating?' Angel purred with rapier-sharp amusement.

Gaby tipped her head back, thinking that Angel in all his bronzed muscular glory was quite exciting enough without a lap dance included. 'Well, we all have our fantasies,' she countered, refusing to rise to the bait.

'Care to share?' he prompted.

'Not right now,' Gaby replied unevenly, keen to change the subject because when Angel mentioned intimacy, however obliquely, he threw her into a quandary because she had still to decide whether or not she intended to share a bed with him again. She liked to think things through but around Angel such straight thinking was a challenge. When she tried to weigh pros and cons into the equation it made her feel petty and appreciate that she needed to simply go with the flow.

'I like your uncle, Prince Timon, very much,' she remarked quietly.

'A less than deft change of topic,' Angel mocked. 'Yes, Timon is a good guy and I was very lucky he agreed to accept the Regency and take charge after my father died. He had a life of his own as a business mogul in New York and he put it aside for several years for my benefit. For a younger brother, who never wanted the throne and barely knew his nephew, it was a big sacrifice. I couldn't have managed without him though, and he taught me a great deal, particularly about business.'

'Yes, you were only sixteen. Losing both parents together must've been devastating for you,' she muttered ruefully. 'I know I've never really got over losing my parents and my kid brother and I was only a couple of years younger at the time.'

Angel reached for her hand and squeezed it. 'I know you were devastated. When you told me years ago, there were tears in your eyes and the way you talked about your parents and little brother made it obvious that you were a happy foursome. Your loss was tragic...'

'Yes,' she whispered unevenly.

'The death of my parents was probably easier for me,' Angel conceded tautly after a long stretch of silence had prompted her to turn her head and look at him enquiringly. 'We weren't a close family. They had their lives and I had mine and, aside from photo opportunities to sell the cosy family concept to the public, I only saw them occasionally when I was home from boarding school.'

Gaby was frowning. 'It sounds pretty cold and artificial.'

'It was.'

'So why did they have you?'

'Don't be naive. My father needed an heir for the throne and once I was born he could relax, duty done.'

'And your mother...you said she didn't like children much?'

'She didn't but I'm not sure my father would have married her if she hadn't got pregnant, so my conception was probably planned every step of the way,' Angel said cynically. 'Her family had married her off to a man old enough to be her grandfather and she wanted out of Alharia…look, I really don't want to talk about this.'

Disconcerted by that blunt admission, Gaby swallowed hard. 'Er… I—'

'You seem to have an incessant curiosity where my family is concerned. I should warn you that there's a lot of murky messy material in my background, not the sort of stuff you would enjoy hearing about,' he assured her pointedly.

Gaby had paled, recognising that she had pushed too hard too fast for him to talk about his troubled background. He wasn't ready yet to talk, to share with her, but time, she reflected, would make him more comfortable with her. Naturally, her curiosity had increased when she'd learned through his half-brother's existence that there was another whole layer to his family circle.

'I'm not a prude,' Gaby murmured tightly, referring to his assumption that she would be upset in some way by what he called 'murky material' in his background. 'Sensible doesn't mean stuffy.'

'A virgin at twenty-four? That speaks for itself. Look in a dictionary and under P for prude you will find an image of someone who looks remarkably like you!' Angel riposted.

'If you weren't driving, I'd thump you!' Gaby told him tartly.

'See...*sensible*,' Angel murmured, soft and smooth as silk, reaching for her hand and bringing it down on a lean, powerful thigh, the strong muscles below the taut denim flexing beneath her palm. 'You can't change what you are at the core.'

'I seriously hope you're wrong in that conviction,' Gaby contended. 'After all, you're a womaniser and I don't want to be married to a womaniser.'

'I made the most of my freedom while I was a single man, nothing wrong with that,' Angel asserted with unblemished cool. 'Now I'm in a different phase of life and I want a successful marriage.'

'That all sounds very good on paper but it's not easy for a leopard to change his spots over the long haul,' Gaby opined, not so easily convinced that he could be a changed man.

'You cherish such low expectations of me, and do try not to refer to our brand-new mar-

riage as "the long haul". That's downright disheartening,' he censured while electric gates
swept back to allow the SUV access to a steep
track lined with trees that arched overhead in
a living canopy.

The track became rough and stony and
passed along the edge of a large lake, also
surrounded by woodland. A sprawling stone
and wood building that looked remarkably
like a large Tuscan farmhouse came into view.
It was very picturesque and not at all what she
had expected of their destination.

'This place hasn't been used much since
my grandfather passed away half a century
ago. My parents weren't into country life. I
did think about tearing it down and replacing
it with something more contemporary.'

'Oh, no, look at those roses!' Gaby exclaimed, already climbing out of the car to
get a closer look at the superb many-petalled
ivory blooms trained to frame the veranda. 'It
would be a sin to disturb them.'

She likes roses, Angel registered, watching in fascination as his bride lifted an almost reverent fingertip to stroke a velvety
soft cream petal. He wondered if she would
ever touch him with the same appreciation
and wondered why he would even want that
from her, why the sight of her hair gleaming

in the sunshine, her delicate profile and the glitter of the dress sheathing those wondrous curves almost dazzled him. Sexual deprivation, he reckoned wryly. He'd be seeing unicorns in the woods next. After all, women *never* dazzled him.

He was not easily impressed by her sex. He knew that very few women could be trusted, for women had let him down time and time again, not least the one who had given birth to him. No, keep it all in proportion, he urged himself. Gabriella was a rare beauty, clever and entertaining and in a decidedly different style from his previous lovers, but she was also completely infuriating on a regular basis.

'There's a rose garden somewhere around,' he proffered vaguely, feeling oddly guilty for that last critical thought as he thrust open the door and urged her inside. 'I used to fish in the lake when I was a boy.'

Gaby stared at the rustic wooden stairs several feet ahead of her and shone her inquisitive gaze round the roomy hall, with its old-fashioned black-and-white photos on the walls and the cosy fireplace adorned with a basket of greenery and a vase of roses. 'It's charming,' she said softly.

A little woman emerged from an ultra-modern kitchen that looked new and bobbed a curtsey. 'This is Viola, Gabriella. She looks after the house while her husband and sons tend the vines. She's a wonderful cook,' he murmured in a low voice, switching to Italian as he told the older woman that she was free to finish for the day. 'Let me show you the rest of the house...'

Upstairs he showed her into a big airy room with ancient floorboards and a high beamed ceiling but while the surroundings were old, the furnishings were modern. Pale green and white drapes fluttered in the cooling breeze emanating from the open French windows. Gaby walked through them out onto a large balcony that literally seemed to be hung on the edge of a cliff to give a fabulous view of the wooded mountain range and the agricultural land spread out in the valley below. 'I feel as though I'm standing at the top of the world,' Gaby murmured appreciatively.

'Apparently, my grandparents stumbled on this place soon after they married. The house was derelict, and they rebuilt it and extended it several times. I imagine the lake sold itself because my grandfather was, apparently, a keen fisherman.'

'But you didn't know them personally,' she gathered, by the way he was talking.

'No, they had my father later in life and had

passed by the time I was born. It's a shame. By all accounts, my grandfather had the stability that my father lacked.'

Gaby tensed as Angel drew her back into the shelter of his body and slowly turned her round. 'There are upwards of sixty hooks on the back of that dress,' he informed her with glittering dark golden eyes.

'I know,' Gaby admitted with a rueful grin as she collided with those beautiful, black-fringed eyes of his. 'But sometimes you have to work harder for what you want...'

'Is that so? You married a guy who likes shortcuts,' Angel told her, sweeping her up into his arms and striding back into the bedroom.

'People who take shortcuts often pay poor attention to detail,' Gaby warned him with dancing eyes as she gazed up at him. 'And you *are* the party who chose the sixty-plus hooks for me to travel in.'

'But I excel at detail,' Angel swore, setting her down beside the bed and embarking on the hooks that followed her taut spine.

All of her was rigid, she registered uneasily, and not with antipathy. In fact, her whole body was tense with a wicked, almost joyful anticipation.

'Am I allowed to take off my shoes, because

they're pinching my toes?' Gaby whispered. 'Or would that spoil the fantasy?'

Angel laughed and lifted her up onto the side of the bed, lifting her skirt to expose her feet. Lean brown hands curved to her slender thighs as she kicked off her heels with a wince, but she was infinitely more aware of his fingers almost absently stroking her skin. He bent to close a hand round one slender ankle and the same talented digits gently massaged her sore toes, slowly and carefully. A soft sigh of relief escaped Gaby and she leant back on her elbows to extend her foot for more of the same treatment.

Smouldering dark golden eyes gripped hers and her tummy somersaulted, heat surging at the heart of her. Her breath caught in her throat as she gazed back at him, mesmerised by the glittering intensity of his eyes set in his lean dark features. That fast she knew she had been kidding herself about having to make a decision about whether or not she would share a bed with him again. She looked at him and she craved him. It was that simple, *that* basic, like the tingling prickling of awareness engulfing her and the surge of blood rushing through her veins, making her agonisingly conscious of certain parts of her body.

'*Theos mou*… I want you,' Angel growled,

hauling her up to him to snatch a raw, hungry kiss awash with so much passion that it sizzled. 'I was burning for you the instant I saw you in the cathedral. You looked ravishing... I couldn't believe you were mine.'

Her lips pink and lush from the onslaught of his, she pulled him down to her and tasted his sensual mouth again for herself, rejoicing in the hard strength and weight of him over her, desperate for that connection. The plunge of his tongue lit her up inside like a firework display and she squirmed, trembling as his fingertips brushed her bare thigh, eased beneath the lace edge of her knickers and stroked the swollen folds between her legs. She jerked, wildly oversensitive to the smallest touch.

'Angel, please...' she hissed, needing more, wanting more with every fibre of her body.

'Detail at which I excel...' Angel reminded her raggedly, tugging her back upright again, turning her around and attacking the hooks afresh. 'I must demonstrate a little finesse.'

He spread back the fabric from her spine and pressed his lips to a quivering shoulder blade. Her breath hitched low in her throat and hung suspended as he released the hooks one by one while trailing his mouth very lightly over the most sensitive span of skin on her back. It was sensual, rawly sexual, everything Angel could promise with one burning look and her body behaved accordingly, her breasts feeling constricted inside her fancy bridal corset, her nipples peaking into tight buds, the dampness of response pooling between her thighs.

As the last hook released he tugged on the sleeves and her wedding dress tumbled round her toes. The faintly cooler air from the open windows cooled her overheated skin. Angel closed a hand round a slender shoulder and urged her back to face him.

'How am I supposed to stay in control when you look like every guy's fantasy?' Angel enquired, a faint flush scoring his high cheekbones as he scanned the delicate palest blue beribboned mini corset, the diaphanous knickers and the suspenders anchored to the silk stockings.

That he could not hide how impressed he was sent a shot of pure adrenalin powering through Gaby's lack of confidence. With one bedazzled appraisal, in that moment Angel made her feel like the most seductive, gorgeous woman alive. 'You don't need to…er… stay in control,' she murmured.

'I didn't the last time,' Angel muttered in a haunted undertone.

A fractured memory of that night crept

back into Gaby's brain, the sort of recollection she had rigorously suppressed for almost eighteen months. But just then she was remembering that wild, seething passion that had gripped them both throughout that night, incomprehensibly rising again and again even when she ached in every limb, even while she marvelled at how utterly compulsive, how driven sex was with him and not at all the less involved, more casual activity that she had once vaguely imagined it would be in her ignorance.

'Yes…but it was…amazing,' she almost whispered, colour warming her cheeks.

His dark golden eyes smouldered like molten honey. 'And for me,' he confessed grittily, as though it pained him to admit the fact.

He disconcerted her then by dropping to his knees to tug down the filmy knickers. Stiff with self-consciousness, she stepped out of them. That night in Alharia, she had not had to deal with the embarrassment of her nakedness, but here it was broad daylight and her body had changed from what it had been eighteen months earlier. Her hips had widened, her breasts were larger, her tummy was no longer perfectly flat and taut while silvery stretch marks and a C-section scar marred skin that had once been smooth.

His long fingers holding her steady, he used his mouth on her heated flesh. A ripple of raw arousal shimmied through her like an intoxicating drug. She told herself she would stop him, because standing there in the sunshine with that happening to her seemed totally shameless, but instead of stopping him her fingers sank into his luxuriant black hair and little gasps of sheer bliss were wrenched from her.

And then, right when she was on the very edge of satisfaction, Angel vaulted upright and lifted her back onto the side of the bed. *'Angel—'* she began.

'I don't want you to come until I'm inside you, *hara mou,*' Angel husked, unzipping his jeans at speed and ripping open a foil packet with his teeth like a man on a mission to win a marathon.

'I'm on the pill now!' she heard herself exclaim as if that were relevant, when really, she thought a second later, it wasn't in the same way because they were married.

For a split second, Angel paused, a frown line dividing his black brows, and then he flashed her a brilliant smile. 'Good to know...' he muttered thickly.

There was a moment when he stood over her, fully erect and ready for action, and her heart thumped so hard she was afraid that he would hear it. The urgency in his every movement only reflected the crazy pent-up need clawing at her. He tipped her back with ruthless hands and sank into her hard and fast and she cried out at the intensity of the sensation, the ripple of response clenching her as his piercings increased her sensitivity.

'Did I hurt you?' he exclaimed, suddenly freezing.

'No!' she gasped frantically. 'Don't stop!'

Angel grinned wickedly down at her, black hair tousled by her fingers. He shifted his lean hips with expert precision, sending delicious feelings tumbling back through her again, answering the hunger controlling her with his own. Excitement laced her pleasure, her heart pounding, her body quivering with surging response. Need was a tight knot deep in her pelvis, pushing her ever on towards fulfilment. As he set a hard rhythm, pounding into her, sensation piled on sensation. Angel had incredible stamina and within minutes an explosive climax took hold of her. With pleasure roaring through every fibre of her body, she cried out and flopped back on the bed, weak in the aftermath.

Angel tugged her up into a sitting position and released her from the corset, rolling down the stockings with quiet efficiency. Then he removed the tiara and the rest of her jewellery and set it aside. 'Are you hungry?' he asked her.

'My goodness, no,' she mumbled, smothering a yawn.

He pulled back the bedding and gently rolled her unresisting body below the sheet. 'Get some sleep.'

'It's our wedding night,' she reminded him guiltily.

'And you've already surpassed my every expectation,' he murmured softly, smoothing her tangled hair back from her brow. 'I'm going for a shower and then I'm coming to bed too. It has been a very long week.'

'Yes,' she agreed drowsily. 'I have to talk to you about Cassia soon.'

Unseen, Angel grimaced, although he could not say that declaration had been unexpected. Cassia had been hostile to Gabriella even at university and possibly it had been unreasonable of him to assume that Cassia's cool assistance would be welcome to his bride. Sadly, there was nobody more efficient or informed on his staff, he reasoned wryly, but that was life. Unlike him, other people let personal feelings get involved and that always caused trouble.

Yet he couldn't be sorry that he had married Gaby, instead of Cassia, who had once looked so perfect on paper. Now he recognised how Gaby's warmth, both as a personality and as a parent, drew him, how stupendous their sexual connection was proving to be and how intriguing he found that lively outspoken independence of hers.

CHAPTER NINE

GABY WAKENED WITH a sense of well-being that was rare for her. It took a minute or two for her to recognise the lovely sun-drenched bedroom and reorientate herself again after all the excitement of the wedding...*and* the night that had just passed.

A dreamy smile curved her relaxed face, and she shook her head, thinking of that middle-of-the-night passionate encounter and suppressing a sigh. It was only sex, she reminded herself doggedly, and Angel had always excelled in that field. It didn't mean anything either and she needed to remember that the same man had blackmailed her into marriage. It didn't matter that he had had good intentions when he had utilised such pressure and intimidation.

Feeling a little less relaxed and forgiving, indeed annoyed that Angel could so easily make her forget what was truly important, Gaby sat up.

'Oh, good, you're awake,' Angel remarked from the doorway, startling her.

'What time is it?'

'Half-ten…you've slept twelve hours…aside from the occasional waking moment,' Angel rephrased with an utterly mesmerising sensual smile.

Staring at his lean, darkly handsome features just a heartbeat too long, Gaby turned her head away as she scolded herself for being such a pushover. But there he stood, her new husband, and he was strikingly, rivetingly spectacular, lounging there in the doorway without a care in the world, casually clad in a black open shirt and tailored chinos that accentuated every sculpted line of his lean, powerful physique. If she was a pushover in his radius now and again, she thought ruefully, at least she had some excuse.

'Alexios?' she queried anxiously. 'Is he here yet?'

'Marina's bringing him this afternoon. Right now, all you have to worry about is coming downstairs to eat. Since we skipped dinner last night, Viola has made a banquet for breakfast,' Angel explained. 'And it will be served on the terrace behind the house.'

Gaby scrambled out of bed and streaked into the adjoining bathroom and then streaked out again, still naked, to grab a suitcase in search of clothes.

Angel swept it out of her hand and planted it down on the luggage rack by the wall. 'Viola will unpack everything for you. We may not have a full staff here, but you don't need to do everything.'

'I'm used to doing everything,' Gaby muttered, suddenly alarmingly aware of her nudity and wondering how she had contrived to forget that reality for even a minute. She rummaged through the case, located a sundress and vanished into the bathroom, taking in a deep breath only once she was alone again. Then she thought of that 'P for prude' crack and pulled a face at her own reflection. In time she would get more comfortable with that kind of intimacy, she reasoned ruefully.

When she emerged again, the bedroom was empty, and she went downstairs where Viola was waiting, her smile widening in delight when Gaby addressed her in Italian. The older woman showed her out through a door onto what Angel had referred to as a terrace, a misnomer if ever she had heard one, Gaby reflected in wonderment as she scanned her surroundings. Stone pillars ran along the rear of the house, marble stretched below her feet and fabulous classical frescoes adorned what had once been the back wall of the house. It was incredibly theatrical and unexpected and Gaby grinned.

'I can see that, in spite of appearances at the front of the house, your grandparents brought the palace here with them,' she remarked with a smile as Angel rose from a low wall to greet her arrival.

'Viola told me that while my grandfather was in his library, my grandmother spent her time out here painting and working on garden projects.'

'Viola's worked here for a long time, then,' Gaby commented. 'Did you visit this house as a child?'

'Marina brought me here to go fishing and run wild in a way that I couldn't at the palace. Even when I was a kid, I was expected to behave like an adult there,' Angel admitted, pulling out a chair for her at the table that was swiftly becoming laden with the variety of options Viola was wheeling out for their delectation.

'Weren't your parents here as well?' she asked in surprise.

'No, but I often brought schoolfriends here with me.'

As his lean, darkly handsome features tightened and shadowed, Gaby's brows pleated. 'And what was that like?'

'Usually good fun with little adult intervention. It was different once I was older.' Angel fell silent and looked out to the garden as though an unlucky memory had stopped him dead in his tracks. She wondered what that memory was and what had triggered it, wondering if it might explain Angel's lack of trust in women, wondering if one of the schoolfriends had actually been a youthful *girl*friend. Sooner rather than later Gaby intended to find out, but she would take one small step at a time.

Like the 'terrace', the garden was much more elaborate than one would have expected from the farmhouse setting. A riot of roses grew round a central fountain while box-edged beds were planted with herbs and perennials and paved paths ran between. Across to one side and screened off by a hedge, she saw the pale watery gleam of a swimming pool.

'It's really beautiful here,' she said, keen to move on from the family and schoolfriends topic, which had silenced him. She knew enough to surmise now because, clearly, Angel hadn't enjoyed a family life with his parents or a happy childhood. Either his parents had been too detached in nature or too busy as the sovereigns of Themos to spend much time with him.

Angel smiled again and she knew that changing the subject had been a tactful move, even if curiosity needled her more every time she had to do it. She had not known that Angel could smile at her as much as he did, and she liked that change. Angel had always struck her as rather dark and reserved at his core, rather than open and smiley.

She ate with appetite, helping herself to tasters from various plates and giving him a running commentary on her preferences while he ate only fruit, finally admitting that he had breakfasted around dawn, being an inveterate early riser, no matter how tired he was or where he was in the world. Seated dreamily in a rocking chair in the shade, Gaby sipped her coffee, pleasantly replete from the meal.

'So,' Angel murmured softly. 'Cassia?'

And Gaby almost choked on her coffee. 'Yes, that topic's likely to be pretty difficult to tackle,' she mumbled in an awkward recovery.

'Why should it be? Cassia is not good with other women, but she is exceptionally good at what she does at the palace,' Angel opined.

Gaby stiffened at his supportive, approving intonation when referring to the blonde. 'Did you ever think of marrying her?' she heard herself ask rather abruptly.

Taken aback in turn by that sudden question, Angel frowned. 'In these circumstances I would like to say no, but it would be a lie. For a couple of months before I met you again, I did consider Cassia as a bride because I've never wanted an emotional connection with a woman,' he explained curtly. 'I don't feel anything for her and I'm not particularly attracted to her, but I did think she would be a suitable choice for the role of future queen... and then you came along.'

'And Alexios came along,' Gaby filled in, striving to conceal her dismay at what he had told her, which meant that on that score, at least, Cassia had not been lying. At some stage, the blonde *had* been in the running to be Angel's wife and she had been astute enough to guess that fact without him ever voicing the idea.

'It *was* merely a thought,' Angel extended as if he sensed her unease. 'I didn't mention the idea to her or indeed ever let our relationship become close. Once one crosses those boundaries with a member of staff it is impossible to step back.'

Some of Gaby's healthy colour had returned to her cheeks and, indeed, she even contrived to smile at him. 'So, you've never had sex with Cassia?' she double-checked.

His frown darkened. 'Of course not. What is this all about, Gabriella? I'm beginning to feel as though I'm on trial for something.'

Gaby raised an anxious hand. 'No, no, absolutely not! But this topic and your explanation does lead into what I had to discuss with you relating to Cassia,' she framed uncomfortably. 'Yesterday, on the very day of our wedding, Cassia told me that you and she were lovers on an…er…casual basis and that that would be continuing *after* our marriage…'

Angel sprang upright, golden eyes gleaming dark and hard as jet with astonishment. 'She's an old friend. Are you sure you understood her correctly?' he shot at her.

Gaby was knocked off balance by that immediate expression of doubt and his grim change of mood. 'Yes, I understood her perfectly. Maybe you don't *want* to believe me, Angel, but she *did* make that claim before the wedding. I'm sorry, but I don't lie about stuff of that nature.'

'I didn't accuse you of lying,' Angel countered tautly. 'But in my experience, women often do tell lies about each other.'

'And now you're just showing your prejudice,' Gaby told him, a chill running down her spine even if, unusually for her with Angel, she retained her calm. And she knew why: she was in shock at his flat refusal to credit *her* side of the story.

Angel spread two lean hands in an expressive arc of disagreement and dismissal. 'I can accept that you don't like her and that you don't want to work with her. However, I've known Cassia since childhood, and I have never known her to be less than truthful.'

'So, I'm the liar.' Gaby framed that obvious deduction with gritted teeth.

Angel shrugged an unapologetic shoulder and turned on his heel. 'Let's not go there. I'm going out before I say anything that I will regret,' he bit out. 'I'm disappointed in you, Gabriella!'

'Not half as much as I'm disappointed in you,' she riposted, and for a split second she simply sat there before she plunged to her feet and grabbed up her phone.

'Angel!' she called, racing after him because he was already halfway out of the heavy wooden front door.

His arrogant dark head turned, and he shot her a winging glance as though incredulous at her audacity in daring to approach him again after what he had said.

'I want you to listen to this…' she murmured quietly as she opened her phone and extended it to him. 'But, in the mood that you are in, *not* while you're driving.'

'I am *not* in a mood,' Angel bit out from between white even teeth.

He was struggling not to lose his temper. It was written all over him from the flush on his exotic cheekbones to his fiery gaze right down to his knotted fists. He had ridiculously expressive body language and she wondered why it was that, even when she was mad as hell with him and reeling with the hurt that he had caused, she still just wanted to soothe him much as if he were Alexios.

'What is…*this*?' he questioned rawly, grudgingly accepting the mobile phone.

'It's a recording of the conversation that I had with Cassia. No, *I* didn't record it… I'm not that quick off the mark or suspicious. It was Laurie who recorded it. When Cassia asked to speak to me alone Laurie didn't trust her and she left her phone recording in the bedroom with us,' Gaby advanced stiffly.

'How sordid,' Angel pronounced with slashing distaste.

'You know what?' Gaby elevated a dark

coppery brow. 'Sordid or not, I'm belatedly very glad to have the proof of that conversation when evidently I married a guy yesterday who doesn't believe a word I say,' she condemned as she walked away again.

'Gabriella—?'

Gaby spun back, blue eyes flashing as bright as the sapphires she had worn the day before. 'I've said all I want to say for now. But when you return, I will be getting some things out in the open for your benefit,' she warned him curtly before she walked back outside again.

She was shaking like a leaf from the amount of emotion she was holding inside herself. She reached for her coffee again, but it was cold. Viola appeared with a fresh pot and began to clear the table, occasionally shooting troubled glances at Gaby's pale set visage.

'He was a very unhappy little boy, ignored and neglected by his mother,' Viola whispered in Italian. 'And a temper like...like a firework display!'

'I can imagine that,' Gaby commented, striving to relax sufficiently to smile reassuringly at the older woman while tucking away those nuggets of information. He must have been so hurt and damaged by that maternal negative response, she thought unhappily. The same woman who had abandoned Saif as a baby had been no warmer a mother to Angel and yet she had had every opportunity to be a parent to Angel. The first woman who should have loved and nurtured him had refused to do so. Was that why he found it so hard to trust people?

Even *her*? His new bride? Angel had blindsided Gaby and plunged her into shock. He didn't trust her. He might have married her, but he didn't have any more faith in her word than he might have had in a stranger passing him on the street and that *hurt*. In addition, he only trusted Cassia more because he had known the woman for years.

That was a moment of revelation for Gaby. She thought about that non-disclosure agreement she had refused to sign at university even though it had meant that she'd lost any chance of being with Angel. Why hadn't she recognised then just how deep Angel's distrust went? There it had been, a blatant signpost, and yet she hadn't seen his fatal flaw. How stupid and naive was she?

He trusted Cassia more because he had known her from childhood and had presumably never witnessed Cassia's less attractive flipside. For that reason, when he heard that recording, he would be abashed, she reflected without pleasure. But regrettably for Angel it would only figure as one more piece of proof that *no* woman in his life could be trusted…

Angel drove up to the mountaintop viewpoint and parked. He was in a rage because he had believed that Gabriella was superior to the other women he had known, too honest to malign an employee who had once offended her, too decent to use her newly acquired status against someone who could not fight back. When would he learn? he asked himself angrily as he climbed out of the car with the phone, ignoring the bodyguards spreading round the car park to protect him. He had worked out when he was very young that the only person he could fully rely on and trust was himself.

He hit the play button on the phone, lean dark features tense and dark and brooding. He listened and the angry flush on his cheekbones slowly drained away. His lush black lashes hit his cheekbones as his lips parted on an unspoken but vicious curse. The whole truth and nothing but the truth…even if it was an *ugly* truth? He knew he had dug himself into a very deep hole. A taxi hummed at the entrance to the car park, doubtless eying the flag on the SUV that signalled Angel's presence. He sprang upright and swung back into the SUV to drive down the mountain again.

Back at the house, he strode into his grandfather's library, needing the familiar warmth of its seclusion and the aged whiskey in the crystal decanter. He poured himself a drink and knocked it back with unusual enthusiasm. It still didn't wipe out the image he kept on seeing of the dead look in Gabriella's beautiful eyes and her pallor. He breathed in slow and deep while the heat of the alcohol burned the chill from his chest. He had screwed up. Why did he always, absolutely *always* screw up with Gabriella?

And as he paced the floor, it seemed so obvious to him why things went continually wrong with Gabriella. His childhood had screwed him up. In any relationship with a woman, he would always be waiting for the axe to fall, and so he had avoided relationships altogether once he'd left his teens behind. All because his mother had been a cold creature, more interested in her latest lover and the beautiful face that met her in her mirror than in her own flesh and blood?

Angel knew right then and there that he didn't want to go through life refusing to have faith in others. What sort of an example would that set his son, Alexios? Alexios, in his innocence, had offered his father instant love and trust. And if he wanted to be the father and the husband that his wife and child deserved, he had to open up and share his past to give his trust as well.

Gaby sat down to lunch alone. She had no appetite, but Viola had been so attentive that she felt that she had to eat lest she hurt the older woman's feelings. Mostly she had sipped her wine, relieved to feel a little bubbly boost from the alcohol when the rest of her felt as flat as a pancake. She wandered round the paved garden with her glass, enjoying the sunshine warming her skin and settling down on a stone seat with beautiful roses blooming all around her.

She heard the crunch of Angel's footsteps on the gravel before he moved onto the paved path and her slim shoulders squared.

'Will you come into the house so that we can talk?' Angel enquired quietly.

'I really don't think that we have anything to talk about,' Gaby parried, fixedly studying the rose bed directly ahead of her.

'Please…' Angel planted his big strong body in front of her view.

It was a word he rarely employed and he got points for it. In any case, she knew they had to talk even if she didn't see what exactly they could discuss. 'There's not very much to say about your prejudice against women,' she murmured flatly.

'I have my reasons.'

'Reasons you won't share,' Gaby cut in.

'I will. I will talk freely,' Angel asserted, crouching down in front of her, endeavouring to enforce eye contact. He reached for her hand, but she yanked it back and he sighed. 'I haven't been in what you would call a relationship before, not a proper one. I *will* make mistakes because I haven't got that experience.'

'You've been with more women than… probably Casanova!' Gaby condemned wildly, wrongfooted by a humble approach that she could never ever have expected from Prince Angel Diamandis. 'Don't try to make a lack of experience an excuse!'

Accidentally, she connected with tawny black-fringed eyes that were the purest gold in the sunshine and her mouth ran dry.

'That was sex and only sex, *not* relationships,' Angel specified tightly.

Gaby flushed with pleasure at that admission and slid upright. 'OK.'

He walked her silently indoors to the library she had heard about and not seen, and it was as much of an anomaly in such a house as the classic frescoes painted on the rear terrace. It was two storeys tall with a spiral staircase in one corner. Customised carved wooden bookshelves covered every wall, and the shelves were packed, upstairs and on the mezzanine above. Sumptuous sofas, armchairs and a large desk completed an ambience that would have been more at home in a Victorian mansion. And yet that very unexpectedness made her like the house even more and wish that his grandparents had survived for her to know them, because she was beginning to understand that the farmhouse had been their escape from the Aikaterina palace, a private place where they could be themselves and indulge their interests like private citizens rather than royals.

'It's very comfortable in here,' she remarked, sinking down on an opulent sofa covered with striped pale green velvet and liberally fringed and tasselled.

'I find it very hard to trust people.' Angel leant back against the desk, visibly striving to look relaxed but taut as a bowstring to her more discerning gaze, every line of his lean, powerful physique tense. 'It probably started when I was a kid. My mother didn't have time for me or interest in me. She lacked the maternal gene, if there is such a thing.'

'I'm sorry,' Gaby almost whispered, reluctant to interrupt but needing to express sympathy.

'But possibly the most damaging event for me happened when I was fifteen…' Angel's voice trailed off and he compressed his wide, sensual mouth. 'It is hard for me to tell you something I have never shared before with anyone.'

Gaby sat in the suffocating silence waiting while Angel collected himself like a male about to climb a challenging mountain.

'I brought my best friend back to the palace for the summer vacation and she…she seduced him—'

'She…*what*? How old was he?' Gaby broke in, utterly taken back.

'He was fifteen too. I found them in bed together and afterwards when I tried to confront her, she said, *What did you expect when you brought home such a beautiful boy?* She had neither regret nor shame.'

Gaby had paled as he'd spoken, and she didn't know what to say. It was too shocking and disgraceful for her to label or contrive some trite remark, because nothing could soothe such a betrayal for an adolescent boy, or the adult son who still cringed recalling that distasteful experience.

'I shouldn't have been surprised. I was aware of her many lovers. She was a great beauty, but she was a heartless mother,' he proffered stiffly. 'I have not shared these facts with Saif…and would like your promise that this will remain a secret, because I see no reason to distress him now with the truth about our mother.'

Gaby gave a vigorous nod and muttered, 'Of course. I won't ever mention it to anyone.'

'That is probably where what you see as my lack of trust began,' Angel continued tautly.

'Probably,' Gaby conceded uncomfortably.

'Then the very first woman I slept with sold the story of our encounter to an international tabloid newspaper, and several after her did the same. That was when I began to look for signed non-disclosure agreements to protect myself,' Angel framed grimly. 'My parents were surrounded by sleazy rumours and conjecture for the whole of their reign. There was a lot of truth in the sleaze, but I wish to create a different image for Themos. I did not want that smut and sleaze and gossip to damage the kingdom's reputation.'

A knock sounded on the door and Angel stalked impatiently across the room to answer it. While she could have suspected some irritation on his part as Viola bustled in carting a massive tray, he, instead, took the tray from her and thanked her warmly. He settled the tray on the desk and sighed. 'She knows I missed lunch so she *has* to feed me.'

'She seems very fond of you.'

'Yes, the older staff who work for the family were the parents that my own parents couldn't be bothered to be,' Angel explained wryly. 'I was very fortunate to have them and I am equally fond of them. They went beyond their jobs to show me interest and kindness.'

Gaby got up to pour the coffee and pile sandwiches on a plate, which she extended to him. 'Yes, I'm helping feed you!' she said tartly. 'I haven't forgiven you yet, but I am starting to understand where and why you started thinking the way that you do. The real problem, though, is that you keep on making me pay for your past experiences and, regardless of what a bad time you've had with other women, I'm not prepared to accept that *I* have to pay for *their* sins.'

'And I don't expect you to,' Angel assured her. 'I have to change my outlook.'

'It's not that easy to change your basic nature,' Gaby cut in, unimpressed.

'It's lot easier if you can see that you have continually *wronged* someone else, particularly someone who has never given me cause for such distrust,' Angel disagreed, giving the words emphatic weight.

Disconcerted by that frank little speech, Gaby sank back down on the sofa. 'Continually?' she queried that use of the word.

'I may make mistakes but I'm not stupid, *hara mou*,' Angel contended. 'We didn't get together when we were students because of my lack of trust, but I'm a little more mature now, although looking back on the way I behaved when you tried to tell me that you were pregnant, that maturity wasn't on view.'

Gaby suppressed a deep sigh of relief that he had truly begun to examine the way he had always treated her as though she were as untrustworthy as some of her predecessors.

'So, you see, you *can* teach an old dog new tricks,' Angel murmured with wry self-mockery. 'I can change. I can see when I'm being unreasonable now…because it's you.'

'And Cassia…?' she prompted uncertainly.

Angel munched through a sandwich in reflective silence. 'She'll have to leave our employ. I was really shocked by that conversation. Thank Laurie for recording it. I would never have dreamt that Cassia would tell lies like that. I did have total faith in her as an employee, but what she said… I'm sorry that I gave you the impression that I trusted her more than I trust you, because that is untrue. I simply had to think it through.'

'But the recording helped and hit home like a sledgehammer,' Gaby gathered with hidden amusement as he wolfed down another sandwich and she refreshed his coffee.

Her earlier sense of despair was gone. Angel was more emotionally intelligent and stable than she had believed he was, but her heart ached for the betrayal his mother had visited on him. He was damaged by the indifference and betrayal of a nasty mother and a succession of lovers, who had wanted him for his status and wealth and had then used him as a publicity tool to enrich themselves.

'What I regret most…is that day you came to the hotel to tell me that you were pregnant, and I refused to listen,' he confided heavily. 'That mistake cost us both so much. All that was on my mind was the number of other women who had claimed to have conceived by me and had lied. In the following weeks I did become more rational and appreciate that I had reacted that way because I assumed you were lying as others had before you and that that belief upset me…and in some way prevented me from taking a more logical approach.'

'I do understand that,' Gaby murmured ruefully. 'Even at the time I understood that, but I also assumed that you wouldn't want anything to do with our child anyway.'

'I'm a possessive tyke when it comes to anything belonging to me,' Angel confided with a gleam in his beautiful eyes. 'I was searching for you within days of that blasted meeting that went so wrong. I was so angry with you. I still don't understand *why* I was angry with you.'

'Surprises are a challenge for you?'

'No. Is it possible for us to start again with a fresh page?' Angel asked, lacing his long fingers with her shorter ones.

'I don't see why not,' Gaby conceded unevenly, emotion surging as she looked at him, another revelation infiltrating her awareness. She still loved him and the more he told her, the more he talked, the better she understood why she loved him. He had his faults, just as she had, but they were working through them. They were both older and wiser and Angel was being forced to share a lot more of himself with her, but she wasn't about to tell him that she loved him when he had told her that he didn't seek an emotional connection with a woman. She desperately wanted to ask him why he had said that, but she reckoned that he had already had quite enough of such stuff to discuss that day, without her choosing to add another complication that he had to explain.

'I want to kiss you…' Angel told her huskily, feeling as though a great weight had fallen from him, relief and a sense of peace assailing him and a whole rush of other feelings he couldn't label following in their wake. 'But I don't know if—'

Gaby took the cup of coffee out of his hand and set it aside with confidence. 'You're a miracle worker. A couple of hours ago, I wanted to run away or push you off a cliff and now… I want to kiss you back.'

'If I'm honest, I want a hell of a lot more than a kiss,' Angel confided raggedly, his smouldering golden gaze telegraphing a hunger she understood right down to the marrow of her bones.

'Kind of guessed that.' Gaby laughed, recognising that they had moved a major obstacle in the path of their relationship and were already moving on in a better direction. And for Angel, she realised, renewing physical intimacy after all that emotional intensity was a much-needed release.

'A sex strike would be very effective on me,' Angel confessed with sudden appreciation.

Her nose wrinkled. 'Kind of guessed that too.'

Angel vaulted upright and pulled her with him across to the staircase in the corner. 'Takes us straight upstairs,' he told her with a wickedly sexy grin.

CHAPTER TEN

ALMOST TWO WEEKS LATER, Gaby traced idle fingers across Angel's bronzed chest. 'So, this not seeking an emotional connection with women,' she mused as lightly as she could in tone. 'What's that all about? You made it sound like some sort of mission statement.'

Gaby wanted to know if she could ever be honest with him about how she felt about him. Or would her feelings always have to be a secret?

'It was. It came from seeing how my father was affected by my mother. She ruined him. I think he loved her, but she wasn't the sort of woman who made a man better and stronger for caring for her...and he was rather a weak man.' Angel rested his head back on her lap, black lashes almost hitting his cheekbones as his long lean body stretched in relaxation. 'I was told by a reliable source that his lifestyle only became as debauched as hers once he realised that she would never be faithful to him. Just think of how much better a man he might have been had he fallen for a classier woman.'

'Yes, but that was him and you said he was weak. Nobody would call you weak,' Gaby assured him with shamelessly seductive intent, slender fingers smoothing down over his bare abdomen, hearing the responsive hitch in his breath, fingertips teasing through his happy trail along the waistband of his low-slung denim shorts. 'So, why can't you have an emotional connection?'

'Could be because I'm too busy handling the sexual connection!' Angel teased with a wicked grin, rolling over and back to tumble her down flat on the rug below the trees at the edge of the woodland. It was one of the few places in the grounds of the house that they were safe from any kind of surveillance, although Gaby had heard Angel having an earnest discussion with his head of security about the risk of drones. The chances of anyone catching a snap of her in a bikini or, worse, rolling about half naked with her husband outdoors, were slim to none, she thought fondly.

The days they had spent together since the wedding had flown past at unbelievable speed, packed with outings, time spent with

Alexios, nights of passion and more happiness than Gaby had even known she could feel.

He had taken them out to show them his country and they had travelled back and forth across the island, visiting the the most gorgeous beach, where Angel had built Alexios his first sandcastle and then smashed it flat to make his son laugh. They had dined at a trendy bar above the beach where everybody had watched them covertly, but they had been left in peace, neither photographed nor approached. As Alexios had dozed off in his high chair, she had realised that Angel could go nowhere on Themos without being recognised. They had spent the previous weekend sailing on his yacht with Marina in tow, so that they could go clubbing at the southern tip of the island where there was a very exclusive resort. She had swum, snorkelled, danced, slept for hours both day and night after yielding to Angel's seemingly insatiable appetite for her, and one day had slipped so smoothly into the next that she could not now imagine a life without him.

'You've got to stop trying to play games with me, *hara mou*,' Angel husked, hungrily claiming her pink lips and sending her heartbeat to a racing pitch. He lifted his tousled dark head and, tawny, black-lashed eyes glittering over her, he smiled again. 'I'm a master gameplayer and I will trump you every time. Of *course* I have an emotional connection with you.'

Her face was burning but her discomfiture was not sufficient to prevent her from saying uncertainly, 'You...*have*?'

Angel grinned, pure devilment dancing in his eyes as he coiled back from her and started to gather up the picnic stuff. 'Naturally. You're my wife and the mother of my child. You belong in an entirely separate category.'

Gaby's teeth gritted. It was one of those regular occasions when she still wanted to throw something at him for being the clever clogs he was always going to be. She didn't want to be in a category all on her own, she only wanted to know exactly how he felt about her. She wanted to know his every thought and feeling too, she conceded ruefully, and neither desire was likely to be met.

They walked along the path by the lake until the house came into view again.

'It really enraged me when you accused me of cheating on you all those years ago,' Angel remarked without warning.

Gaby sighed. 'I know that technically we

had broken up and you were free to do as you liked, but I was upset. Who was she?'

'An ex. It went no further than what you saw. I *wanted* to upset you,' Angel admitted, startling her. 'An unpleasant urge to follow, I'm afraid. We were both very young, Gabriella. You, in particular, at nineteen were far too young for me. I may only be a few years older, but I was many years older in terms of sexual experience. You were just a baby in comparison, and you were right to say no to me. I reckon you had more emotional experience then than I had, though.'

'Sometimes you surprise me.'

'In what way?'

'In a *good* way,' Gaby stressed helplessly because she admired his honesty as they walked back to the house by the side of the lake.

Marina was in front of the house, sitting on the grass with Alexios, and Gaby's son lifted his arms and loosed a baby shout when he saw his parents.

'I *love* being appreciated,' Angel admitted, closing an arm to her spine. 'Can I tempt you into having a second child with me yet?'

Shock stilled Gaby in her tracks. 'Why?'

'I missed out on so much the first time around.'

'And it was all your own fault—an *own goal*, I think you could call it,' Gaby pointed out gently. 'And no, it's too soon for me to consider another pregnancy…maybe next year.'

Just thinking about the concept blew her mind. Was she really that secure that she could even consider another baby? She couldn't demand love from him as though it were some kind of right written into the marriage vows, could she? Self-evidently, Angel wanted their marriage to work, and he wanted it to last. He had put in the effort, baring his soul of his worst secret to explain why he suffered from such distrust. With that one act he had blown a huge hole in her defences.

Gaby believed that Angel had been more sinned against than he had sinned. The mother who should have loved him had instead withheld her love and attention and had then let him down unforgivably by succumbing to lust rather than considering or even respecting her son's needs. He was ashamed of both his parents, ashamed and filled with distaste and regret for the different experiences other adults had with their closest relatives. At least she had warm loving memories of her parents, she reflected ruefully. Until Angel had told her about his childhood, she had not fully appreciated how lucky she was to have had fourteen years with a caring family.

They had only just stepped indoors when his mobile phone began ringing. As she carried Alexios upstairs for his bath, she heard his voice take on a clipped cold edge that was unfamiliar to her and she wondered if something had gone wrong back at the palace. Angel had made several trips back to meet obligations that could not be cancelled, and although she had offered to accompany him he had always refused, telling her that she would have her own schedule and duties to fulfil soon enough.

'The Crown council want the Coronation held within three months and that will keep us busy for weeks,' he had pointed out. 'When we get time off, we take it, and I don't want you feeling like you have to spend less time with our son.'

There was a terrible irony to the reality that she now understood exactly *why* Angel had insisted on marrying her. Sadly, that truth hurt. His childhood had been quite miserable. Materially he had had everything, but emotionally he had lived in a wasteland where only his parents' employees had brought warmth into his life. As a result, Angel was determined that Alexios would have a much more positive experience, which he believed entailed two caring parents and stability. Angel set a very high value on a mother's love. So, he had married her for their son's sake, and he would *stay* married to her for their son's sake, so naturally he was inclined to look on her a little as though she could be a baby dispenser. Having discovered to his surprise that he adored his son, he was now keen to encourage Gaby to give him another child.

With Martina's efficient assistance, Gaby bathed Alexios and got him tucked into his sleepsuit, ready for his supper. When she walked back into her bedroom, she was surprised to find Viola already packing for her, for they had not planned to return to the palace until the following evening.

She went downstairs and discovered that Angel was still on the phone. Suppressing a groan, she grabbed a coffee from the machine in the kitchen and walked out to the terrace. Clearly there was some sort of crisis and they were leaving sooner than they had expected.

'What's happening?' she asked as Angel strode out to join her.

'An almighty mess,' he told her grimly, his beautiful mouth compressing. 'We'll discuss it on the drive back to Aikaterina.'

Within twenty minutes they were on the

road. Gaby cleared her throat and shot a bemused glance at Angel's tense profile.

'Cassia is in a cell at police headquarters,' Angel revealed, staggering her with that news.

'But what on earth—?'

'The waiter serving you at that restaurant the night you were drugged went missing and, when the police tracked him down, he confessed that he had been given the pill and paid to drop it into your glass of champagne,' Angel explained tautly. 'His bank account contained a substantial sum of money and when the police "followed the money", as they say, it led straight to Cassia. She was arrested. Supposedly she intended you no real harm. She expected you to collapse under the influence of the drug, and look like a drunk or behave in some foolish way that would embarrass you, and therefore me as well, in public…'

Gaby's eyes were huge. 'Good heavens…' she whispered in shock. 'And what was she hoping to achieve with that? That you would cancel the wedding? Turn your back on your son? I don't think so.'

'Whatever Cassia's intentions, I now have to find a way to deal with this problem, and without blowing apart the rest of my household staff. Until I've had more time to think,

Gabriella, I can't discuss this further with you.' Angel abruptly drew their conversation to a close and resumed his brooding demeanour as he stared out of the window.

Gaby felt stung that he'd shut her down so decisively. This involved her. She was the one who'd suffered at Cassia's vindictive hands. She had every right to demand that Angel share his plans for dealing with Cassia with her. How could she ever believe that they could have anything approaching a real marriage if, even after baring his soul and seemingly accepting that she would never hurt him, Angel was still shutting her out? After all their talks over the last couple of weeks she'd felt so sure that they were starting to really connect, that maybe he could fall in love with her as she had fallen so deeply in love with him. But the moment something like this happened—something big—Angel was reverting to type.

And as angry and shocked as she was at Cassia's actions, a tiny part of her felt some sympathy for the woman—after all, hadn't she thrown all of her usual caution to the wind as she'd allowed herself to be swept up in the whirlwind that was Angel? Who could better understand Angel's powerful draw than herself? Look at the lengths she had gone to to experience even a slither of his attention. She'd married the man—and not because she'd had to, but, she freely admitted now, because she was in love with him. She knew all too well the pain of loving a man who would ultimately never let himself love her back. Cassia had very obviously had deeper and more enduring feelings for Angel than anyone had realised in order to have gone as far as to drug his fiancée two days before her wedding!

They passed the remainder of the journey in stony silence, and, with Alexios sleeping peacefully in his car seat, Gaby didn't even have the comfort of her son to distract her from her increasingly despairing thoughts. She now saw that she had a decision to make. Stay in her marriage to Angel and break her heart over him, or leave and break her heart anyway...

The moment they pulled up at the palace, Angel leapt from the car, his mobile phone pressed firmly to his ear as he marched inside and disappeared, leaving Gaby to get herself and their son out.

Gaby had spent what felt like hours holed up in the nursery with Alexios and Marina, struggling to distract herself from her spiralling thoughts concerning Angel and the future of their marriage. She wondered what was being discussed, what decisions were being made on her behalf. Would he ever tell her just what went on behind those closed doors?

The door to the nursery opened and Angel appeared.

He asked her to join him in his wing of the palace.

'*Your* wing?' she questioned, it not having occurred to her before to have wondered where his bedroom was. 'I assumed we'd be sharing.'

'Which I was about to suggest,' Angel volunteered as he walked her along the wide, high-ceilinged, hugely imposing picture gallery that connected the two different sections of the palace. 'My parents occupied separate wings.'

'And you were on the top floor, all of you nicely separated,' she commented.

'That's how they lived but it's not how I want to live,' Angel admitted bluntly.

His crest would have risen in her eyes had it not been for his brooding silence in the car, and the spiralling, panicked thoughts it had triggered in her. How was she supposed to know how Angel wanted to live when he never properly opened up to her? But dared she hope that was about to change? Nervous beyond belief, feeling her future happiness at stake, she couldn't help but notice that the wing that he inhabited was much more formal and traditional with oil paintings on the walls and grand antique furniture. 'You'll have to give me a tour of this place. I had no idea that this side was so different from mine. I've seen the public rooms downstairs, of course.'

'We only use the ground-floor reception area for major events and, since times have changed and people have become more egalitarian, I don't use them half as much as my parents did.'

He showed her a room off a long wide marble-floored corridor. 'I thought the nursery could move in here and we could have Alexios closer to us…there's rooms for the staff as well.

'This is the sitting room,' he told her, standing back to allow her to admire a giant expanse ornamented with formal drapes and a massive marble fireplace. 'It should be dragged into this century, like a lot of the accommodation in this wing. But I'm not interested in the décor, so I'm hoping you will step in…'

'It's possible,' Gaby commented, not wishing to give a definitive answer as yet and commit to a move within the palace. She'd not even decided if she could stay in the marriage yet. What had been decided about Cassia?

'This is the master bedroom…and it connects with another bedroom, which you could use as a dressing room or whatever.' Angel studied her fixedly, a frown line starting to pleat his brows. 'You're very quiet.'

'You've obviously done a lot of thinking about this rearrangement, but right now I'd prefer to talk about Cassia and why you went so broody and quiet on me in the car after telling me she was the one who drugged me,' Gaby confessed ruefully, wandering across the huge gilded room with its ridiculously majestic bed on a low dais, which was surrounded by gilt pillars. It was a level of splendour and magnificence so far removed from her experience that she felt intimidated. Slowly, she turned back round to face him.

'Seriously?' Angel grimaced. 'I've spent half the day having to talk about Cassia, with her parents, her friends, her colleagues—it's been endless. I've had to be polite, tolerant and compassionate when only a couple of centuries ago I would more happily have stuck her in a dungeon in the basement and had her executed…and, to be quite frank, *that's* the endgame I would've preferred!'

Astonished by that shattering declaration, Gaby gaped at him, blue eyes very wide.

'Well, how do you expect me to feel?' Angel demanded. 'You could have had an allergic reaction to the drug, could have been seriously harmed by it, but Cassia didn't care,' Angel bit out. 'I think she simply wanted to hurt you because you were marrying me. I am stunned that I failed to appreciate, in all the years I have known her, what a scheming, vindictive woman I had working for me!' Angel exclaimed harshly. 'How did I *not* know? How could I have been so blind to her real nature?'

'She wasn't family or your girlfriend,' Gaby proffered. The depths of the turmoil Angel was finally sharing had her instinctively looking to comfort him. 'I suspect that you never looked that closely at her. She's poisonous but I don't think men find that trait as easy to spot as women do. So what *will* happen to her now?'

'I want to keep a lid on this whole toxic mess. I want to ban her from Themos, which, believe me, will be punishment enough.'

'You don't want her charged?' Gaby countered in surprise.

'Ultimately, as the injured party, the decision is yours. If you want her in court, you must make that choice.'

Gaby breathed in deep and slow. 'But you would prefer to brush the whole thing under the carpet?'

'I wouldn't have put it in those words but, yes, that is the preferable option in my opinion. If we prosecute her, it will hit the press. I don't want to treat the world to the story of my bride being roofied before our wedding. Regrettably, in our circumstances and with my reputation, nine out of ten people will assume that I was having an affair with Cassia and that sordid interpretation will accompany us all to our graves. Clearly, Cassia was violently jealous of you.'

'And very possessive of you,' Gaby filled in. 'I think she truly believed that she would end up as your wife. Had believed that for many years.'

'Unfortunately, most people will believe that she had cause to be jealous even though she didn't. I do want her punished, but in a manner that also respects her family's service to the throne and removes her from Themos and your radius,' he extended gravely. 'Her father, Piero, is a long-standing family friend and a very decent man. He and his wife are in pieces over their daughter's treachery, but your safety must come first. If Cassia went to prison she would be out again within a few years. As it is, in return for her confessional statement, I will remove her citizenship and she will not be able to get back onto the island.'

Gaby nodded comprehension.

'That is my preferred solution because I never want to lay eyes on her again in this lifetime,' Angel continued with grim intensity. 'It protects her parents' reputation and residence here as well. They are wealthy and can maintain contact with their daughter however they wish in the future. I could never forgive her, though, for what she did to you...*that* could have had a tragic conclusion!'

His dark deep drawl roughened as he finished speaking and she gazed across the room at him, momentarily entranced by the volatile liquid gold of his gaze, sensing the powerful emotions he was restraining.

'I'll go with whatever you choose,' Gaby responded with a sigh. 'A scandal would be embarrassing, and *if* she went to prison—'

'Oh, she would *definitely* go to prison on Themos,' Angel incised. 'Buying a banned drug and using it to assault my bride? She has broken several laws and the charges are serious, not inconsequential.'

Angel fell silent then and Gaby could feel the despair in him, which made her wonder if something else was wrong. 'Angel, is there something else I need to know?'

'You were targeted *because of me*. Your life was put at risk *because of me*.'

'That's not how you should view her unbalanced behaviour.'

'No, but it's the bald, unlovely truth!' Angel sliced back harshly. 'I had a dangerous employee, and I didn't realise it. Not only didn't I realise it, while I was refusing to give you my trust, I was giving *her* my trust and regarded her as a friend! Cassia could have *killed* you with that drug!'

'Luckily, she only gave me a headache,' she said soothingly.

'Luck doesn't count when it comes to your safety,' Angel informed her. 'You mean the world to our son and to me, *hara mou*. Anyone who wishes you even the smallest ill is unwelcome on Themos.'

Surprise filled Gaby, swiftly followed by pleasure.

'I let you down with Cassia and I feel so guilty about that,' Angel exclaimed abruptly, disconcerting her. 'I let myself trust her rather than you...you, who have never done a single thing to inspire distrust!

'I couldn't have survived you being hurt,' Angel confided, stalking closer, his brilliant gaze intent. 'I need you to be happy and content here in the palace, living on Themos with me...'

Gaby could feel her heart beating very, very fast, as if she were on the point of starting a race. 'Why?'

'You know why,' Angel told her confidently. 'You own me body and soul. Why else were you asking me about why I had never wanted an emotional connection with a woman? I'm in love with you. I've probably been in love with you since you were a student, only I couldn't feel safe with you then without an NDA and I turned my back on you...but I never forgot you for so much as a week at a time. I tried to find you in other women, and I couldn't...'

'Oh, my word,' Gaby whispered, in so much shock that she actually felt dizzy.

'Is that *all* you've got to say?' Angel exclaimed.

'I had no idea that you loved me,' she muttered unevenly. 'No idea at all. I had hoped that you might come to fall in love with me, because I've been in love with you again since the wedding... I don't know how, though—it's not like you deserved love after forcing me into marrying you in the first place. But I do love you, flaws and all.'

'That was a kind of backhanded declaration,' Angel complained with his usual arrogance. 'You wouldn't have married me if you hadn't secretly wanted to. You're a tough cookie. You would have fought me to the last gasp if you didn't want me as well.'

Gaby looked reflective and then nodded grudgingly, because there was a certain amount of truth in that accusation.

'*Theos mou*…we're almost fighting about it!' Angel carolled in disbelief as he grabbed her up in his arms. 'You crazy, wonderful woman! I love you to hell and back.'

'It's to the moon and back,' she corrected.

'No, it *was* hell when we were apart. We had those few weeks and I felt so alive and impossibly happy when you were around, and then it all vanished as though it had been a dream,' he confessed in a fracturing tone of regret, his dark golden eyes full of turmoil as he remembered that period. 'I was miserable without you in my life.'

'That NDA,' she reminded him gently, but she was not as unhappy as she should have been to hear that he had been miserable without her. 'You broke my heart.'

'Broke my own too, but I don't think I was ready to commit to our future back then,' Angel told her ruefully. 'And you were too young and naive to handle me, but it's not like that any more.'

'No, it's not.' Gaby could barely credit what he was telling her, but a ball of warmth was expanding inside her chest and it was happiness, joy, all the things she had assumed she would never be able to feel with Angel except in fleeting moments. But what he was offering her now was so much more. Love would keep them together through the tougher times. Love would embrace Alexios in a cocoon of security as well. She smiled.

'You don't throw things now, you talk, you clarify,' Angel pointed out lethally.

'Keep quiet or you'll put me in a bad mood,' Gaby warned, trailing off his tie, embarking on his shirt with even more enthusiasm.

'Does this mean you're planning to move into my bedroom?' Angel husked.

'It's under consideration,' Gaby countered, not wanting to give away her every advantage at once.

'How hard do I have to work to get what I want?'

'I should think you'll be very busy persuading me tonight that having you in the same bed has benefits,' Gaby told him impishly, her sapphire eyes full of tender amusement.

Long fingers framed her vibrant face and

he looked down at her with an adoration he couldn't hide, which lit her up inside like a torch. 'I love you so much, *asteri mou*…'

'My star?' Gaby translated. 'Good grief, you can be romantic.'

'Wasn't it romantic when I asked you to keep on the wedding gown and the sapphires?' Angel complained.

'No, that was you living out a fantasy, but I was still underestimating you then. You were trying and I didn't see it. You were right. My expectations *were* too low,' Gaby confided, wrenching him out of his shirt with a huge smile, struggling to come to terms with the concept that Angel Diamandis was, finally, absolutely hers. 'I will never stop loving you.'

'I won't let you stop. You have a lifetime ahead, which you will share with me and our family. For the first time ever, I have a family and I will do whatever it takes to keep it,' Angel swore fiercely, and then he gathered her into his arms and passionately kissed her breathless. 'Right now, we're going to celebrate.'

'Bossy…much?' Gaby asked.

'Secretly you like it,' Angel told her, his lean dark devastating features illuminated by a charismatic smile.

'Just you keep on telling yourself that. I

love you *in spite* of your bossy taking-charge ways,' Gaby informed him.

'I just love you because you're beautiful, fierce, clever and sexy,' Angel murmured thickly as he tugged her down onto his opulent four-poster bed with sensual urgency. 'Note that I'm not criticising anything.'

'Hush,' Gaby urged, resting a fingertip against his parted lips as she gazed lovingly down at him. 'You make me incredibly happy...'

'We have a whole lifetime ahead of being together, *kardia mou*,' Angel savoured, tugging her inexorably down to him, stretching sinuously over her, all hot, sexy masculinity and unafraid to show his arousal.

Gaby emerged flushed and breathless from a passionate kiss. 'What about dinner? Won't the staff—?'

'They'll wait until we call...perks of royalty.'

'Or being a ruthless operator,' Gaby slotted in before he kissed her again and her worries about being more polite and considerate with the staff melted away, because when she was with Angel, nothing, absolutely nothing else, mattered and she too wanted to celebrate their new happy togetherness.

EPILOGUE

Six years later

'THEY'RE ALL DOWN?' Angel murmured quietly from the doorway. 'Even Castor?'

Gaby grinned at him from the side of the cot where their youngest child slumbered. Even at ten months old, Castor was very different from his older, more tolerant brother. Castor had a shocking temper when life didn't go his way and he only slept when it suited him. He didn't like strange faces, unfamiliar places or different food. Keeping their baby boy content entailed effort.

'Fresh air works magic,' she said, and the King and Queen of Themos, both dressed down for their stay at the lake house in the mountains, walked to the door of the bedroom next door, where four-year-old Eliana slumbered, her shock of copper hair as bright as her mother's, her lively blue eyes shut, fast asleep after a day racing through the woods in her big brother's wake.

Alexios was dead to the world, sprawled out across his bed as though he had been felled there. Gaby lifted the tablet that had fallen from his hand and set it aside. He was her firstborn and she couldn't credit now that he had ever been a baby because he was so big and likely to be even taller than his father when he reached maturity. He looked like his father, but he had the temperament of neither parent. He was intelligent and thoughtful, an energetic boy but slow to anger and very patient.

'He really enjoyed you taking him fishing this morning,' Gaby told him as she closed the door.

'No more about the kids,' Angel growled, nipping at the skin between nape and shoulder and sending a thrilling pulse of desire thrumming through her. 'Saif and Tati will be here soon with their crew and they'll be jet-lagged and they won't settle for hours.'

'Stop complaining,' she scolded. 'You love seeing your brother and his brood.'

'It's our wedding anniversary. Remind me why we wanted to entertain other people?'

Angel urged, guiding her into their bedroom with single-minded intent.

'Because Saif and Tati are the only company we have that we can totally relax with,' she reminded him softly, because it was true. They could say whatever they liked in company with family, for there was no fear of saying anything that might offend or be controversial or appear in the press, and that was probably one of the reasons that the two couples had become such close friends. It didn't hurt that they were all young and had children in the same age group either. In addition, Gaby had become very fond of Saif's down-to-earth wife, Tati.

'You're right. I'm being selfish because when I finally get you all to myself, I don't want to share you with anybody, even… *Theos mou*…my own kids.' He groaned as he pressed kisses across her bare shoulders, tugging her shirred sundress down to expose her unbound breasts, cupping that soft weight with another sound of masculine appreciation. 'This is my favourite dress—'

'Because it comes off quickly. Sometimes you are very basic,' Gaby teased, even as she arched her spine and pushed her taut nipples into his hands, quivering as that touch of abrasion sent a hot dart speeding into her pelvis.

'And you don't like it?' Angel growled, grazing his teeth across her sensitised skin as he backed her down on the bed, shimmying off her remaining garments with sure hands.

'You know I love it…' Gaby looked up at him, her heart in her eyes, an ache stirring at her core as he stood over her, swiftly shedding his clothes, revealing that long, lean, muscular bronzed body that she never tired of appreciating.

'As I love you, *Vasilessa mou*,' he husked, coming down over her, taut and ready for action.

My Queen. Literally and figuratively, that was how Angel treated her. She revelled in the sense of security he gave her every time he looked at her. She had the family she had always wanted, and the wonder was that he had wanted the exact same thing. She saw the tenderness, the appreciation, the unquestioning loyalty that he gave her. And the nights with him were out of the world as well, she reflected, her neck arching with her spine as he sank into her with hot, driving impatience and the excitement took her by storm.

Afterwards, listening to Angel in the shower

when she felt too lazy to as much as shift a toe, she thought about how lucky she was.

Angel was a terrific father, always involved with the children, encouraging as much as he disciplined, understanding when the kids got it wrong, as children so frequently did. He had also been a wonderful supportive guide while she learned how to deal with being a royal consort. Her language skills had proved very useful, and she had been warmly conscious of Angel's pride in her ability. Tati's advice had proved good as well, although the Emir of Alharia lived in a much more formal manner than his younger brother did. Angel had dismantled much of the pomp and ceremony at the palace and embraced a more contemporary style, but Saif didn't have the same freedom because his country was more conservative.

Her friends Liz and Laurie were regular visitors with their families. The previous month they had invited them all to Paris to spend the weekend with them in Angel's fabulous town house there. Saif and Tati had joined them as well and the weekend had turned into a terrific party.

But as a rule, Gaby and Angel found their relaxation as a family unit by spending week-ends alone at the house in the mountains. Free of the formality of the palace and the many staff, they got to be themselves and it kept the children grounded because nobody waited on them at the lake house. That was a much better preparation for the real world than the palace was and taught them some independence. And to her chagrin, when Viola was away on a break, Gaby had discovered that Angel was a much better cook than she was. But then, one of the joys of being married to Angel, she thought fondly, was the number of surprises he could still give her.

'Almost forgot,' Angel remarked as he walked back through the bedroom, showered and fully clad with that leaping energy he never lost. 'For our wedding anniversary...'

'You already bought me that necklace!' Gaby exclaimed, sitting up in bed.

'This is a ring...' Angel informed her somewhat smugly, lifting her hand to thread a diamond eternity ring on beside her wedding ring. 'For ever and ever, you are mine and I am yours...it's engraved on the inside.'

Minutes later, she realised what time it was and fled into the shower to get dressed because Saif and Tati were due to arrive. They were both downstairs as the helicopter came in to land at the front of the house.

'You finally cracked the mould,' she told Angel tenderly. 'That engraving is truly romantic...'

* * * * *

Blown away by
Her Best Kept Royal Secret?
*You're sure to love the first instalment in the
Heirs for Royal Brothers duet*
Cinderella's Desert Baby Bombshell*!*

*Also, don't forget to check out these other
Lynne Graham stories!*

The Italian in Need of an Heir
A Baby on the Greek's Doorstep
Christmas Babies for the Italian
The Greek's Convenient Cinderella
The Ring the Spaniard Gave Her

Available now!